GOODY GOES BAD!

REGGIE CHESTERFIELD

I0566400

ROYAL CHERRY

For BAC, the KOAWD.

Paperback ISBN-13: 978-0-9845418-2-9
Paperback ISBN-10: 0-9845418-2-9

eBook ISBN–13: 978-0-9845418-3-6
eBook ISBN–10: 0-9845418-3-7

This book is a work of fiction. Names, characters, places and incidents are either the product of the author's imagination or are used fictitiously. Any resemblance to actual events or locales or persons, living or dead is entirely coincidental.

1

"I just don't see how people can do that sort of thing to themselves," Annie said as she took a sip of her diet coke. "I just don't see why they would want to."

Alicia nodded uncomfortably. She was starting to squirm at the subject of the conversation which, whenever she was talking to Annie, inevitably led to a girl named Julie with whom they had gone to high school. While she was a little older than them, they had been considered part of the same crowd. In fact, they had been members of the same chapter of Cheerfully Chaste at their church. It was a group that urged young people to stay virgins until they were married. It required them to sign pledges that said that if they ever had sex outside of marriage, they would not only bring shame and disappointment to themselves and their families but would also cause them to be looked upon as no more than common prostitutes. In addition to this, it demanded that do this with a smile and a happy heart. Naturally each meeting would begin and end with the members grinning widely and saying the motto of the club, "I must cheerfully deny myself pleasure."

Since she was a little older than them, Julie had been their mentor. And while all the rest of the girls had gone over to the "dark side," Annie had kept it as a source of pride that she still adhered to the pledge. She, herself, was now a mentor to the girls of the chapter.

It was true that some people might have referred to the members of Cheerfully Chaste as being uptight or goody-two-shoes, however they had always thought of themselves as responsible girls who always did the "right thing" and always "respected their bodies." Julie, however, had strayed from the path and had recently gone on to become the biggest slut in town. This was completely out of character for anyone who had ever been a member of Cheerfully Chaste to even imagine, much less do. At first everyone had thought it was a rumor, but it had actually turned out to be true. Very true. Julie was fucking everybody in town. Even girls. Even black guys. It didn't matter who she did it with as long as she was getting off.

"And she's married now! That's what gets me!" Annie emphasized, probably for the hundredth time. "You would think that she would stop whatever it is that she's doing! But she just keeps…." She paused because it pained her to even say the word. "…*screwing* everything and everybody in town!"

Alicia nodded and tried to feign interest. This conversation was really getting old. In fact it was all they ever talked about any more. She had actually been looking forward to this lunch, too. Cousin Junior's Chicken House was her favorite fast-food joint and she was really getting annoyed by the fact that Annie could not let this subject go. The fact that the guy behind the counter, the assistant manager, kept leering at her didn't make things any easier. It was really distracting. And it was ruining the two piece white snack that she had so been looking forward to.

"I just don't see why she does this to her poor husband. I mean, if he ever finds out, he's going to divorce her! I don't know of any man who would let his wife just have sex with anybody the way he does!" Annie was so angry at this point, she was almost spitting her diet coke across the table. She was that disgusted.

Alicia continued to nod as Annie kept going on about Julie. She and Annie had once been really close friends but lately they seemed to be growing apart. It was like they were outgrowing each other. They both still had a lot in common. They were the same age. They liked to shop. They wore similar clothing. They went to the same college. They were around the same size. They even looked like a matched set except Annie was blonde and Alicia was a brunette. It was just that there was something that wasn't clicking anymore.

"Are you even listening to me?" Annie said as she took a breath from her ranting.

Alicia started. "Yeah , sure."

"I don't mean to keep going on about her, but I think it's just a shame what she's doing. I mean she was one of us. I used to look up to her and now she's just giving her body away to everybody. She broke the pledge. Doesn't she remember what it means to say, 'I must cheerfully deny myself pleasure?'"

"Maybe you should talk to her?" Alicia timidly suggested.

"Oh, I have. I saw her wasting her money on a scratch-off at the convenience store and believe me, it was not pleasant."

"What did she say?" Alicia asked curiously.

"Well, let's just say that she was not apologetic at all. She doesn't feel bad at all about what she's doing. She said that she loves, and I quote 'sucking big cocks and eating pussy' and that she has never felt better about it in her life. And you know what she said when I brought up the chastity pledge?"

Alicia looked at her. She already had an idea of what she said.

"She said 'F the pledge. Except she didn't say F, if you know what I mean."

Alicia started to squirm a little bit more.

"And you wouldn't believe what she said when I asked her about her husband and what he thought about all this."

"What did she say?"

"She said that he knew all about it and that he was the one who had her turned out in the first place!"

"Really?" Alicia said, starting to get interested.

"Well, I know she was lying and told her so and you know what she did then?" Annie paused for just a second but didn't give Alicia a chance to answer. "She invited me back to her place for a threesome with her husband and then she rubbed my boobs!" She said this with a flourish that can only come from moral outrage.

"Did you go with her?" Alicia asked half-joking.

"Of course not! I'm not a pervert!" Annie said irritatedly. What's wrong with you? And then Julie kept going on about how good I looked and how nice my boobs are just to butter me up, but I was having none of it."

"Well, you do have nice boobs," Alicia said. She was telling the truth. Annie was one of those skinny girls with hips who actually had big breasts. Men would salivate whenever she walked by because they were so big and well-shaped. While her own breasts were very nice and also elicited a lot of stares, Annie's were the type that people fantasize about. Men and women. Man, they were huge.

"What? These big old things!? They just get in the way! I'm thinking about getting them reduced. I mean a natural E cup? Who would want these things?"

Annie continued to rant and rave until they finished eating their food. Alicia mainly nodded throughout the mainly one-sided conversation. She was thinking about Julie too, but not in the same way that Annie was. Her mouth was watering at the very thought of what Julie was doing. She could feel herself heating up at the very idea of sucking the cocks of strange men and all that other sexual stuff that was now Julie's life. If only Annie knew what she had been up to lately, then it really would have hit the fan. The fact that she got so horny she couldn't see straight whenever the subject came up was another reason why she didn't want to talk about it with Annie. In addition to making it hard to concentrate on her chicken, it also gave her the added temptation of giving her true feelings away. She was so wet that she was having a hard time keeping her hand off her pussy. She knew that she would definitely have to masturbate in the car.

They emptied their trays and walked to the parking lot. It was an extraordinarily hot summer day and both of the girls couldn't wait to get to their cars and turn the air conditioning on.

"I know you're tired of hearing about it but she just isn't what she said she was. She's just not a good example. She broke the pledge and it just bugs me," Annie added as they parted ways. "See you later!" she said and gave Alicia a little hug. Alicia hugged her back too, getting slightly aroused as Annie's large breasts pressed against her smaller ones.

They each walked to their separate cars. Annie had to get back to her part-time file clerk job at a law firm and Alicia had to get back to class. She was making up some classes that summer because she had taken time off her sophomore year to mentor orphans in the Congo.

Alicia waved as Annie sped off in her Civic. She understood that the thing with Julie bugged Annie. It bugged her too but for different reasons. It bugged her that she was wasting time listening to this goody-goody tell her what was right and what was wrong and judging other people just because they didn't think just like her.

She got into her Subaru and started it up to get the air conditioner going. But before she could get going, she had to pull up her skirt and rub herself. She was so turned on by all the talk of Julie's sex-ploits that she had to start masturbating. She was already wet so she was able to cum fairly quickly, tasting herself as she fingered her shaved pussy. She concentrated on her clit and inserted three fingers into her wet vagina. Even though there wasn't anyone in the parking lot, it just felt so good doing it in public. It was just so freeing not to care about the opinions of others. Even though she wasn't really quite ready to be as open about her sexuality as Julie was, at this moment she did not care what anybody thought. She orgasmed shortly thereafter.

After she had regained her composure, she put the car in gear and drove towards her apartment. However, she had barely left the parking lot when her cell phone rang. Speak of the devil; it was Julie. And she wanted her to come over.

That evening, Annie stood at the kitchen sink washing the remainder of the dishes from supper. She had cooked meatloaf and had invited her boyfriend, Jimmy, over. While she had thought it might look a bit improper for him to come over to her apartment un-chaperoned, she had rationalized that most of her neighbors probably would either still be out committing sinful acts or would be too drunk to notice and misunderstand such a potentially moral transgression. She didn't really know for certain if her neighbors were alcoholics or not, but she had seen them drinking beer one night, so she just figured that they probably were. Well, she had seen *one* of them drinking a beer and had included all the rest of them in her judgment since they all seemed to be friendly with each other. She also doubted that any of them ever went to church. She thought that her assumption was a fair one.

"One drink and you're done," she always said whenever offered a drink. "You're ruined. You take a drink and the next thing you know, you're taking your clothes off and swinging from the chandelier." She had heard this phrase often from her mother, the overriding influence in her life.

Annie's mother was the most important person in her universe. Annie did whatever she said and always tried to avoid doing anything that her mother would judge her negatively over. Annie's mother was a domineering type of woman who many people thought was the most pious woman around, possibly who had ever lived. She didn't smoke, didn't drink and always did everything right. She never said a curse word and the very idea of Annie skipping church on Sunday was enough to send her to the emergency room. She expected Annie to tow the line and people expected Annie to be just like her mother.

"My Annie has never said a curse word," her mother would proudly tell strangers. "And she had never even smelled alcohol."

Most strangers would think that this was a little weird, but they just accepted that Annie and her mother were so good and so pure that it was normal for them to be this way. Annie's mother thought that people who didn't go to church were bad and that people who went to church were good regardless of what they did in their personal lives. It's just the way it was and, if you didn't agree with her...well, then you would suffer your consequences in hell.

Annie's boyfriend Jimmy went along with this life of purity for the most part even though he didn't really have much of an opinion either way. He realized that a guy like him was lucky to have such a hot girlfriend even if she didn't put out. He could handle a lot of craziness just to be the envy of every guy that saw them together. Besides, her extreme views didn't really contradict anything that he did anyway. Even though he wasn't particularly a church going person, he worked at religious bookstore so any sort of drinking or behavior like that was frowned on by the management and his coworkers. He didn't like alcohol anyway because he said it "didn't taste good," but he could sure drink the sweet tea. He would put it away by the quarts. One of his favorite things to do was to eat a whole chocolate cake and wash it down with a gallon of sweet tea. Or if he didn't have any sweet tea, a gallon of milk. He also farted a lot due to all the bad food he ate. His friends referred to him as "Ol' Stinky." Behind his back, of course. Secretly, Annie was a little disgusted by him, but she didn't say anything. Jimmy was a pretty good boyfriend overall, even though he was usually too engrossed in looking at muscle magazines to really have too much of an opinion on anything except to say, "Look at how ripped this guy is, Annie! Wow!"

Jimmy did have a fine eye for the male body, Annie thought. Some of the guys he would show her would have made her mouth water if she had been susceptible to that kind of lower thinking. Especially this one extraordinarily muscled up black guy named Harold Hercules that Jimmy seemed particularly fixated on. But sometimes she did have a hard time looking past the gigantic bulges that almost every weightlifter seemed to possess, especially Harold. If she didn't stop herself, she would begin to feel herself fantasizing about the outline of what had to be their massive cocks. Her nipples would even get hard but that was as far as she would let it get. She would find her large breasts heaving at the thought of being taken by these muscle-bound men and she would find her hand creeping down her skirt. But she would always stop herself. She wasn't that kind of girl and she would not let herself have those kinds of thoughts no matter how much the idea might have appealed to some kinds of women. She was better than that. She would remember that that she had to cheerfully deny herself pleasure and that's what she would do.

"I think something is up with Alicia," she said as she put away the last plate. "She's acting funny."

Jimmy didn't answer.

"Aren't you listening?" she asked, a little perturbed.

"Oh, yeah," he said as he looked up from his magazine. "I was just reading about this new muscle building program. I'm going to try to start putting on some bulk." He flexed one of his thin arms to emphasize what he was talking about. In addition to being able to drink vast quantities of sweet tea and milk, Jimmy was constantly talking about exercising and working out even though he never actually exercised or worked out. He was a twitchy, scrawny guy and frequently talked about bulking up even though he didn't really have anything to bulk up. He was naturally skinny and was under the impression that because one could look at him and see every muscle and vein he possessed that he was "all cut up," as he liked to say. It was true that occasionally, every six months or so, he would give the fellas at work a few pointers on working out or lifting weights but this was as far as his exercise regime went. It was almost as though reading the muscle magazines was exercise enough. And perhaps, to him, it was.

"I mean, this whole Julie thing has my blood boiling. I mean who does she think she is? She's just having sex with everybody. She used to be our mentor in Cheerfully Chaste and she taught us that sex is wrong. That it was something that only dirty people do. And now she's doing it! And with anything that moves!" With that she threw her dish rag down. "It just makes me so mad!"

"Is Alicia angry too?" Jimmy asked absentmindedly.

"That's what's irritating me about her. I don't think she is," Annie said. "She keeps telling me to calm down and to not worry about it." She took a deep breath. "I just don't know about her anymore."

"Well, Julie is a grown woman and can do what she wants," Jimmy added without thinking.

All of sudden, the room grew deathly quiet and everything became still. Jimmy knew that he had screwed up. He flinched as Julie quickly turned around and narrowed her eyes at him.

"Well, that's just the point. She is doing what she wants to do. And it's just not right. She's out there having a good old time while the rest of us are doing what's right and trying to set good examples as women. It makes men think that all women are like that."

"I'm sorry, I didn't mean…"

"I know what you meant," she hissed at him. "You probably wish *she* was your girlfriend. You and Alicia both. Sometimes I think I'm the only one in this world who cares about people doing what's right anymore."

He cowered from her and hoped that she would calm down.

"But that Alicia. There's something going on. She's changed. There's something about her that I can't put my finger on."

"What's she doing?" Jimmy asked hoping to change the subject.

"I don't know. She's dresses differently for one thing. She's wearing short skirts and I could swear the other day that she wasn't wearing panties."

"Really?" Jimmy asked, his interest piqued.

"Yes, perv. It's disgusting," Annie said angrily and shuddered. "She's always distracted too. Like she's thinking about something else."

"Well, maybe she's under stress at school?"

"It's possible, but I don't think that's it. It's like she's…and I don't want to sound weird about this. It's like she's checking me out. It's like I sometimes catch her looking at my boobs."

Jimmy looked up with surprise. "What?"

"I shouldn't have said anything"

"That does sound a little weird," he said.

"I know. Also, her mom said something weird the other day to me at church. Of course, Alicia had skipped again. She never comes anymore. Anyway her mom said that she wished that Alicia could be more like me. And she said it right after we had our Cheerfully Chaste meeting."

"So that's a good thing, right?" Jimmy asked, his eye wandering to the very ripped stomach of an Australian weight lifter who was giving details of his award winning muscle-building regimen in an exclusive article.

"Yes, it is. But it was how she said it. She acted like she thought Alicia wasn't going along with the program anymore. Like she wasn't ever going to Cheerfully Chaste again. It was like she was no longer honoring the pledge. It was like she didn't know that Alicia and I were the only ones from our class still carrying the banner."

"Maybe it's nothing," Jimmy said.

"It probably is," she said and sighed. "Do you want some more sweet tea?"

"Would I ever!" Jimmy said. "And I'll take some ice cream too if you've got it."

Annie groaned inwardly as she went towards the refrigerator. If Jimmy wasn't such a wholesome guy, he would be insufferable.

3

"Oh, shit! Oh, shit!" Alicia exclaimed as the big cock plowed into her. She lost her breath as she came for third time. The tattooed muscular guy behind her didn't let up. He was like a machine and just kept hammering. Wham! Wham! Wham! They were on the rug in the living room of Julie's house and fucking like dogs. After she came that time, she put her focus back on what was going on in front of her. Julie was being screwed missionary-style on the couch. Her legs were up and her eyes were blissed over. Her gorgeous nipples were erect and her neck was flushed. She was truly in sex heaven.

The funny thing was that Alicia had no idea who these guys were. They had been trimming the trees on the street outside Julia's house and she had invited them in to cool off and have something to drink. It was an extremely hot day after all and was the right thing to do. After she had gotten them inside, she had called Alicia and asked her if she wanted to come over. Julie hadn't said anything about sex at this point, but the implication was there especially after she had explained the situation to Alicia. Of course, Alicia couldn't resist. This was her thing now and she would not let an opportunity for good hot sex go by.

Julie's guy kept banging her automatically, his big dick pumping her like a piston in an erotic internal combustion engine. Just watching the rhythm of them fucking was making Alicia hornier and hornier. She thrust against the guy behind her, trying to get even more traction. He responded in kind and amped up his already hard pace. She could feel her body quiver as she began to cum again. She thought about when she had been sucking his cock earlier. It had been massive. He was covered in tattoos and had almost completely shaved his body. He was still a little bit sweaty from working outside. It was almost too much for her to think about and her mouth began to water at the thought of first looking at him. He had been rough with her at first, sucking her breasts hard. Her nipples had ached with excitement and she had been dripping with anticipation at the very idea of having him inside of her.

They continued to fuck for a little while more, but soon Julie wailed as she came again and her guy pulled out of her. "I'm going to cum!" he yelled and squirted all over her cleanly waxed pussy.

She laughed and put her finger in it and tasted it. "You taste pretty good for a tree trimmer."

She moved over to where Alicia was still fucking and sat down in front of her. "Want a taste?" she said as she pushed fingers into the cum and then put them in Alicia's mouth. Alicia hungrily ate the cum and then pushed Julie down and started eating her out. Julie moaned as Alicia licked the cum from her pussy and then began to suck on her clit. Alicia hungrily ate her as she continued being pounded from behind. She licked Julie's breasts and sucked her nipples while inserting two fingers into her drenched snatch. Soon Julie was cumming again and the guy who was ramming Alicia could handle it no more. He pulled out and, not wanting to miss a single drop, Alicia turned around and grabbed his massive dick and sucked as he blasted his hot semen against her tonsils.

"Damn, girl!" the guy said as he finished. Alicia just grinned.

"Now, isn't this a lot more fun than Cheerfully Chaste ever was?" Julie cackled.

"I'll say," one of the tree trimmers said. "My mom forced me into that when I was twelve." Then he started walking around like a robot repeating, "I must cheerfully deny myself pleasure. I must cheerfully deny myself pleasure." He then grabbed his semi-hard dick and started pretending to mechanically jerk off.

Alicia and Julie cracked up. Julie had addressed the comment to Alicia but was happy to see that yet another graduate of that awful program had seen the light.

"Man! This was some hot fucking!" the other one said exuberantly. "You girls need to come over to Cornbread's place some time. He's always throwing a party. People get drunk and fuck and have orgies. It's some really hot shit."

"Cornbread?" Julie asked. "What kind of name is that?"

"Cornbread Pritchett!" The other one exclaimed. "You know him! You know him! Everybody knows Cornbread!"

"I don't know him. And with a name like that, I'm not sure I would want to," Julie said.

"You know him, don't you?" the other one eagerly asked Alicia. "He's rich as hell and he knows how to party!"

Unfortunately Alicia did know Cornbread. Or she knew of him at least. He was the sleazebag nephew of Cousin

Junior Osgood, the man who had started the Cousin Junior's Chicken House Franchise. He was a big, over-testosteroned, red-haired musclehead/redneck who was always jerkassing around town acting like he owned the place. Which he sort of did, since his uncle was the richest man in town.

"His uncle Junior is so rich, he's got a refrigerator just for his cigarettes!" the first one said as though this was a true indicator of wealth.

"Wow," Julie said disinterestedly.

Alicia couldn't agree more with Julie's indifference but didn't say anything.

The biggest problem with Cornbread was that he was an absolute douchebag who thought that he was God's gift to women. He was a cute guy and had the muscles and the tattoos, but he was just such an egomaniac that it turned her off. It didn't matter if he did drive a Corvette and have a big lake house. Personality went a long way with her. However, now that she heard about these parties, and the fact that orgies were involved, maybe there's more to him than she had at first thought.

"I've heard of him," Alicia said at last.

"You would love his house," the first one said. "I mean, it's a party two-four-fucking seven!"

"And that sonofabitch is hung!" the other one said. "I mean, he gets so much pussy that there's always plenty to go around!"

Alicia thought this sort of adoration of Cornbread's endowment made him sound a little bit like Annie's boyfriend, Jimmy, but kept this to herself.

"Maybe Cornbread might be the kind of guy I need to meet, after all." Julie said.

"Maybe so," Alicia added. Now that was she getting turned out, there might be something to be said about a guy like him. She didn't have to necessarily like him to fuck him.

It might be good. Especially if he was as hung as this guy made him out to be.

"Yeah, he is! I mean when you show up at his place, you had better be ready to leave your damn clothes at the door because that's where they'll eventually end up! Everybody has a good time at Cornbread's!" the other tree-trimmer said emphatically.

"You don't even have to be invited! Pretty girls can just show up! Cornbread loves pretty women!"

Alicia and Julie both filed this away for future consideration.

They sat around for a little while before the tree trimmers left. With them gone, Alicia felt that it was time to talk to Julie about Annie. She knew that she was somewhat betraying her friend by divulging this information, but Julie was also a friend and she thought it was only right that she fill her in. Especially now that they had so much in common. After all, they had just had a small orgy together.

"Annie always was such a little prig," Julie said. "But then again so was I."

"So what happened to make you change your mind?"

"My husband had me turned out for one thing. But also I guess I just got older. I matured."

"I guess that's what happened to me, too." Alicia sighed. "I mean it happened over time. I just started thinking about it and I realized that it was really kind of weird for a girl in college to still be a virgin. I mean, besides Annie, it seemed like I was the only one."

"You probably were. I had given up my virginity earlier than that, but I never really enjoyed sex until I started letting go and getting freaky," Julie said with a laugh.

"I started hard from the get-go. I mean, once I decided to go for it," Alicia said. "I was sitting around thinking about it when I realized all the adults I knew wanted me to be like them. I mean, it's like as they get older, they become more like adolescents. It's like they're in their forties but they act like they're twelve years old. They don't smoke. They don't drink. They act like they don't even know what sex is. They just sit around talking about their gardens and how pure they are. It's just so weird. They even collect dolls and baseball cards!"

"I know! Those people at that church are always talking about how grand they are and how they're just not interested in 'things of the world' when you know they're all just a bunch of perverts."

They both laughed.

"I just had enough one day," Alicia said as she continued her explanation. "I was tired of being like one of them so I decided I was going to do something about it. After I got out of class one day, some guys invited me out to a bar and I did everything that I was taught not to do. I drank a lot and got drunk. One thing led to another and I fucked every one of them in the parking lot. I didn't start out to gangbang all of them, but after the first one, I knew that I had to have more. It was like I found out what I had been missing out on and I loved it. "

"Everybody does," Julie said, nodding her head.

"Even Annie?"

"Of course," Julie said. "You see, Alicia, most people want to be sexual. It's just in them. They all want to be out of control. They want to fuck. The wilder the situation, the better. They are just looking for the right place and context. Just look at the people who get busted at swing parties. They always live in regular places and have regular jobs. They're doctors, ministers, teachers. They're just like everybody else. Being like this is in everybody. Most people are just looking for an excuse to get a little crazy."

Alicia could understand that. It just felt so right when she was fucking that she couldn't imagine thinking that it wasn't. But then a thought occurred to her.

"I know," she said. "So, you're saying if Annie had the right excuse, she would get turned out, too?"

"Oh, yeah," Julie said. "Women love to be dirty. We love to do nasty things. We're just looking for the right reason to do them. We all want to be sluts. You of all people know this first hand."

"So how would I go about it? You know, showing her the way?"

"Well, a friend of my husband turned me out. His name was Charlie. He was great. The things he made me do..." Julie couldn't help but get wet at the memory.

"So do you think he could do it for her?"

"No, he had to leave town. He filmed some people fucking at the country club and was going to blackmail them, but it backfired on him."

"How?"

"He thought that he was just filming some people having an orgy, but it turned out they were really filming a gonzo porn movie. Charlie sold what he had shot to some low-budget porn site. When the producer found out about it, he got really pissed off that Charlie had hijacked his footage and was going to break his legs over it. I think that Solid Gold Medallion was the studio he was shooting for. They're pretty big shit."

"Yeah, they are, I think."

"He had to get out of here in a hurry. I don't really know of anyone else besides him."

"What about you?" Alicia asked.

"Oh, she would never let somebody like me turn her out. It has to be someone she doesn't know. She would be too self-conscious with us. Afraid that we would judge her. I would love to eat that pussy though. Mmmm... Besides, I'm going out of town tomorrow."

"Where are you going?"

"Out to California. I'm going to go out and see my friend Josie. You know the one that's dating Brother Red Hair?" Julie said.

"The TV preacher?"

"Yes. Now he's got the right idea about sex. I'm going to do some work at their Church and then fuck the absolutely shit out of the both of them. My husband Dave is already out there on business. We're going to meet up out there."

Oh, how Alicia envied her.

"Well, do you know of anyone else?"

Julie thought for a second. "I don't really know off the top of my head. All I know is that if you can ever get her to let loose then turning her out will be piece of cake. Everybody wants to be a freak sexually."

"I know. That's the problem though. How?"

"I know from personal experience that the more uptight you are the freakier you'll get. There was this professor who used to come into the library at the college when I was working there. He was a young guy for a professor but he was hung! I mean you could see it through his pants. He couldn't hide it! That big dick of his would even swing whenever he would walk. But he was just so straitlaced. He wouldn't even look at me no matter how much I bent over in front of him or leaned over him. It was just so frustrating because I wanted to fuck him so badly. I watched him for a month and I knew I was going to have to have that big thing one way or another."

"So what did you do?"

"I decided to go for broke. I told him that we had a rare book he might be interested in back in one of the storage rooms. I got him back there and backed my ass up against him. He stiffened up and that big dick of his came to life. I was wearing a short skirt without any panties and I just lifted it up and rubbed my pussy against him some more and nature took over. Before he could run away, I was down on my knees and had that dick out of his pants and sucking it."

"So, you got him past the point of no return?"

"Yes. I knew if I could awaken the pervert within, then there would be no going back. Nowadays he's this big swinger in town. He's so booked up with women wanting that massive cock of his that he almost has to schedule them. And to think he was a virgin before me. "

Alicia thought about it for a minute. "That's what I need to do with Annie. Awaken the pervert within."

"Oh, yeah. She'll open those legs for anybody if you just get her in the right situation."

Alicia thought about it. This would be tough because Annie was so rigid about everything. She never did anything without considering her chastity pledge. She didn't drink and she didn't party. She really didn't do anything. There had to be something, though. Everybody has a weakness.

"Keep me updated while I'm gone," Julie said. "I can't wait to see how this turns out."

"Oh, I will."

Julie leaned over and started rubbing Alicia's leg. "You can do this, Alicia, I know it." Then she leaned in and kissed her. Alicia hungrily kissed her back. But before she could go any further, she paused.

"Julie?"

"Yes?"

"Could you give me the name of that professor? He really sounds like somebody I would like to meet."

Julie laughed. "Of course. That big dick of his will knock your socks off!"

With that she put her hand on Alicia's pussy and started rubbing her already wet clit.

Alicia closed her eyes with pleasure. She couldn't wait to get started on Annie. All she needed was her inspiration.

Annie woke up the next morning and her apartment was absolutely sweltering. Her large breasts were sweaty and her thin night shirt was sticking to her. She lifted up her shirt to let some air on her big tits. The air felt good on them. She thought about taking her shirt off but then realized that her shade was still up. She quickly pulled the shirt back down and hoped that no one had seen her.

"That darned air conditioner has gone out again," she said to herself. But that was no surprise because there was always something going wrong with her apartment. She called the maintenance man, David, who finally answered after about the tenth ring. She wasn't surprised. He wasn't exactly the hardest working of individuals but he said he would be up shortly. Luckily she didn't have to be at work that day so she would be there when he finally decided to show up. He always seemed to work on his own schedule.

She took a shower and watched some TV. While she waited she picked up the phone and attempted to call her mother. After trying a few times to reach her, she put down the phone. She didn't know where her mother could be but figured that whatever it was, it was probably somewhere where she could do something holy and good like handing out tracts or chastising sinners. She decided to put on her workout clothes and sat around her apartment for a little while and looked at magazines until the heat became too unbearable. Then she went out to the balcony. It was still morning and the air was much cooler out there. She figured that she would go to the gym after David showed up. If he showed up, that is. She was still consumed by her thoughts about Julie and the potential betrayal of Alicia to let the heat bother her too much. She just couldn't stand the idea that someone would not think the same way that she did. How obvious could it be? Her way was the right way and how dare anyone else think otherwise!

A few minutes later, someone knocked on her door. It was David, the maintenance man. She let it in.

"It's the air again," she said and smiled at him.

While David was known around the complex as the "incredible disappearing maintenance man," she did really like him. He was a very muscular black guy who was always quite friendly to her. He was also really funny. She liked to talk to him because he had a really good attitude about life and always had interesting things to say. Naturally, he had a bad back that always seemed to start bothering him whenever he was asked to help somebody lift something or do anything that might resemble physical labor. Regardless of this disability, he was really good at fixing things.

"Let me look at it," he said, smiling. He hoped that this air conditioner wouldn't be too much trouble to fix. He was really tired and Annie's call had awakened him from a nap. He realized that if it was going to be too much trouble, he could always say that he had to go to the store and get a part. This would allow him to finish sleeping. It was a good thing that Annie was such a hot little piece otherwise he wouldn't have even bothered coming. His eyes looked her over and he liked what he saw. He could feel himself getting hard just at the thought of how her sweet pussy must taste. He also thought about her gorgeous boobs and how good it would feel to put his big dick between them and give her a proper tit-fucking. And that tight pussy! How that must feel! He had long wanted to fuck her, but since he was a professional, he had resisted even the slightest urge to show her this side of himself. Besides, he knew how uptight she was and he did not want to lose another job because of sex. He had been fired from the previous apartment complex he had worked at because he had been caught in a threesome with the owner's wife and secretary. The bad thing about it was that the owner's wife had promised him a new Hyundai and he had had to leave before she had had a chance to buy it for him.

"Sure thing," she said.

He towered over her and she couldn't help but get a look at his very muscular body as he walked through her apartment to look at the unit. His uniforms fit him like a glove due to his fit physique. She found her eyes lingering on his body quite often whenever he was around and sometimes felt herself heating up at the thought of him. Today was especially bad due to the fact that because the apartment was so hot, he was sweating and his shirt was sticking to his well-formed back. She just wanted to reach out and touch him and feel his rock hard muscles. He looked like one of the guys in Jimmy's magazines. Before she did something stupid she made herself look away.

He turned and looked at her. "You getting ready to go to the gym?"

"Yeah, I just wanted to show you what was going on."

He nervously cleared his throat. "I hope you don't think this is forward of me, but you have a really fit body. You ever think about doing any fitness modeling?"

Annie was a little taken aback and flattered at the same time. "No, no one has ever asked me."

"Well, I have a friend down at the gym who has a hook-up with a magazine. He used to play pro football. He does shoots all the time and is always looking for new people. If you want to give it a try, I'll tell him and we can set something up."

"Sounds wonderful," Annie said. She was blushing because like any woman, she was so happy that someone would think that she should model. "Are you sure he would want to take pictures of me?"

"He's shot me a few times and you're in better shape than all the other girls that's been there. He would love you."

"Wow, I'll think about it."

David hoped so.

"Yeah, we used to play football in high school together. I could have gone on to the pros too, but you know, I've got this bad back and besides, I figured that I didn't need all that mess. I mean, traveling and all that. I had bigger goals than that, you understand?" David said. "I wanted to help people and shit on more of a street level."

Annie had heard this story regarding David's football days about a dozen times before except sometimes the reason why David hadn't gone pro was because of his mother needed him to stay home and sometimes it was a bad knee. Sometimes it was because the coach didn't like him. She listened on. "Wow, that's too bad," she said sympathetically.

"That's the breaks," he said and smiled. While his story was usually all it took for some women to feel sorry enough for him to have sex with him, he wasn't really expecting Annie to ever do this. Just seeing her in a bikini would be enough to keep his fantasies going. On the day of the shoot he would be sure that it was the skimpiest one provided. He would make damn sure of that.

David put his focus on the air-conditioner and peered deeply into the panel. "Man, it is hot in here or is it just you? Do you know if anyone else is having this problem?" he said thinking of a way to stall fixing hers. It was definitely too damned hot to work. "What about your neighbors?"

"I don't know," she said and quickly stopped looking at his broad back. She licked her lips before she could think about it. She hoped he hadn't noticed.

"Why don't you go over and ask them?

Annie hesitated for a second. She really didn't like her neighbors but thought that it might be a good idea to ask them. They were lesbians and Annie did not approve of their lifestyle at all. They were accountants or something like accountants and, even though they drove Harleys on the weekend, they were very much of the lipstick variety. They looked good, so Annie couldn't figure out why they didn't want to get married to men. While Annie had no real reason to dislike them, she just did so on principle. People like her were supposed to condemn and dislike people like them and she was not about to change that. It didn't matter that they had always been nice to her but she just figured that this was because they were perverts and probably wanted to sleep with her.

Unknown to her, Annie was actually right in this regard because as with David, she was the object of many of the lesbians' fantasies. They also knew how uptight she was and this is why they would flaunt their sexuality in her face. They just wanted to annoy her. Regardless of this, she was getting so heated up with David in the room she thought it was probably a good idea for her to get out of there. "I must cheerfully deny myself pleasure," she murmured to herself as she reminded herself of her pledge to stay chaste.

"I suppose I could, she said and took a deep breath and decided to go over to their apartment. She walked over and knocked on their door. They answered after a couple of knocks.

"Hi, Annie," one of her neighbors said as she opened the door. It was April, the redhead. She was completely nude and making no effort to hide her smoking, tanned body. Standing right behind her was Sunday, her bleached blonde partner. She was nude, too. And equally hot.

Annie tried not to look at her boobs, even though they were very well-shaped.

"Is your air conditioner out?"

Sunday put her hands on April's breasts and stomach and started rubbing them. "I'll say it is. We're *so* hot over here."

Annie rolled her eyes. She was starting to get irritated. She knew they were just doing this to annoy her.

"Tell David to come over her and take a look." April said and nuzzled Sunday's neck.

"Okay," Annie said and turned around quickly and left.

She was fuming. How dare they flaunt that kind of behavior in her face! Didn't they realize how wrong they were to act like that?! She stormed back to her apartment.

"Well, is theirs working?" David asked, casually sneaking a peak at Annie's breasts.

"No, they said to come over and look at it," she said, trying to blot the image of the two nude women out of her mind.

David stood up. "Well, let me go take a look."

"But what about mine? Annie asked. "I called you first." Annie.

"Well, yours runs off of theirs so the problem is probably with their unit. If I can get it fixed, then yours will probably start working. The problem is that it's so hot outside that it's really putting a strain on the system."

"Okay."

David walked out. As he went, he turned to Annie. "Aren't you coming?"

"No, I don't think so," she said.

"C'mon. I'll need you to go check on yours and see if I'm going in the right direction when I'm working on theirs."

Annie rolled her eyes. "Okay," she muttered. Surely, the two lesbians wouldn't still be nude with a man coming over.

They walked over to the two women's' apartment. The door was open so they walked in.

"I wonder where they went?" David asked.

Before Annie could answer, they figured it out. They heard the sound of moans coming from the bedroom. Before she could stop him, David walked into the bedroom. There on the bed was April sitting back with Sunday between her legs eating her out.

"Oh, baby," April said as Sunday licked her shaved pussy.

Sunday looked up at them with a grin right before April started to hunch her face. Her mouth was shining from

April's juices. She began thrusting her fingers into April's pussy.

"Yeah, like that!" April said as she obviously orgasmed.

Annie looked over at David who was transfixed at the scene. He just sat there and stared. At one point, April looked over at them while Sunday continued to lick. She then looked at Annie and winked before smiling and closing her eyes in ecstasy.

They're putting on a show! Annie thought with disgust. They're just doing this to get to me!

Suddenly, Sunday sat up and switched positions with April. April dove in with gusto, fingering Sunday's pussy and licking her erect nipples. Sunday's eyes rolled back in her head as April's hand ground into her snatch. The smell of their sex was extraordinarily strong in the room and they were also making no attempt to keep down the noise.

Even though she was disgusted, secretly Annie couldn't help but be fascinated. She could feel herself tingling with the excitement of what she was seeing. Her nipples were beginning to ache and she couldn't help but cross and uncross her legs, fidgeting as she watched the two women have sex. Still her moral outrage was unchecked. She dismissed these sexual feelings and tried her best to glare at them, letting them know that she did not approve. She looked over at David who was still transfixed. Then she happened to glance down at his pants and saw that he was now sporting an enormous erection. It was gigantic and strained the pants of his already tight uniform. She could easily see the outline of the head of his penis through the polyester. Annie tried to look away but couldn't. He was supposed to here fixing the air-conditioner but instead he was watching a sex show. How shameless these women were! Why wasn't he disgusted by this! She sure was, but still she couldn't look away. She wanted to run, but she couldn't. She was too spellbound by what she saw.

It was just a matter of minutes before the two women scissored their legs together and ground their pussies against eache other until they both came. They both shrieked as they tribbed and humped each other to what sounded and appeared like very satisfying orgasms. Annie's mouth began to water. It was almost overload for her.

"Man, that was hot!" David said as he absentmindedly stroked his aching cock through his pants. He was glad that he had gotten up from his nap.

However, Annie didn't see him do this or hear him say anything. She had already run out the door. "I must cheerfully deny myself pleasure! I must cheerfully deny myself pleasure!" she said to herself as she ran back to her apartment.

5

Alicia walked into the Cicero Hall and looked around to get herself acquainted with the place. Even though she had been going to the university for several years, this was the first time she had ever had any reason to go into this particular building which was where the History Department was located. She was a marketing major, after all, and had never had any reason to know anything remotely historical. The building was in the older part of the campus and looked like more of a small castle than it did a building associated with higher learning. Most of the other buildings on the campus were in the standard-issue seventies-era academic style and were so bland that it was hard to find any interesting architectural detail at all. Cicero Hall was different, however, and was a source of pride for the campus as well as the town. It had also been renovated recently through a grant from the guy who had played Cicero in the TV series *Cicero*. He was an overweight James Coco-type who had created the title role which consisted of him, a full-grown man, portraying a bratty sailor-suited child. It catered to the more mainstream and, to him, less sophisticated, audiences. Needless to say, it was a wildly successful program. However, because he had always thought it was beneath his Shakespearean training that he had become famous for playing an overgrown child, he was always looking for ways to make his legacy less TV related. In other words, he wanted to be remembered as a great thespian—not as Cicero. Oh how he would bristle whenever someone would yell his catchphrase at him, "Hey, Mama! Bring your baby boy some dinner!" This is what drove him to these types of projects. However, sponsoring the restoration had not helped alleviate his feelings of inadequacy. Especially since they had renamed the grand old building after the character that he was always trying to escape. He just couldn't win.

But all this was unknown to Alicia as she became oriented with the building. She then started descending the steps to the office of the professor that Julie had told her about when they had fucked the tree trimmers. Maybe he could give her some insight as to how to get Julie turned out.

She kept walking down the stairs until she finally reached the cellar of the building. There, among the storage rooms and excess filing cabinets, she spotted his office door. She hurried over to it and knocked. He answered almost immediately and she was happy to see that he had been waiting for her. At first glance he didn't look like much. He was tall and skinny and wore oversized bad clothes and horn-rimmed tortoise-shell glasses. He was even wearing corduroy which was weird because it was the middle of the summer. His look was topped off by a bowtie which really looked of place because this guy was probably only in his early thirties. His office also looked like a disaster had hit it. It was filled with papers and historical knickknacks. As well as a lot of dust. She had taken so much care in how she had dressed that day, too, with her short skirt and white top. She realized now that she could have worn anything by the way this place looked. And how badly he was dressed.

"You're Alicia?" he said as he smiled broadly and welcomed her in. "Julie told me all about you." His eyes were all over her and she could see from the rising protrubance in his pants that he was indeed very happy to see her. "Want to hear a joke?" he said suddenly.

"Sure," Alicia said a little taken off guard.

"Did you hear the one about horny Hiawatha?"

"No," she said.

"He got in his canoe and shot off across the river," at this he guffawed. "One of my friends in the English Department told me that one."

"Oh," Alicia said forcing a laugh. She hadn't gotten it but didn't want to hurt his feelings.

While at first she had been a little uncomfortable with the idea of being alone in such an isolated part of the building with this strange man, the size of his penis was reassurance enough that everything was going to be all right. Also, he had led with a joke which was always good. Besides, Julie had vouched for him and she seemed to know what she was talking about when it came to stuff like this.

"You're the professor I've heard so much about. I can say that Julie was right about that." Alicia said and pointed to his erection.

"It is rather big or so I've been told," he chuckled nerdily. He then licked his lips. "Well, Julie told me that you were one hot girl and she was right."

"Thanks. Your name is Richard, right?" she said, focusing only on his straining corduroy pants. She absentmindedly touched her nipples. They were hard and she knew that they would have to come out of her top soon.

"Yes, it is. You can call me Ricky though. People seem to like it better at the swing parties. They relate to it better, I think. It gives me cred." He started chuckling again.

"I think I can see that," she said. She hadn't been to a swing party yet, but from what she had seen from the ads on the internet what he said made a lot of sense. "So what are you a professor of?" she asked and squirmed a little bit, her pussy was getting wet and she was going to have to have that big cock inside of her. But she thought it would be polite to get to know this guy a little better."

"The Ancient World with an emphasis on Babylonian Astrology."

"Hmmm…I see," she answered not really paying attention. Stuff like that just went over her head.

"Do you mind if we lock the door?" he said and cleared his throat. "I think I would really like to plow your fertile crescent like an ancient Minoan."

She looked at him blankly.

"That's a little history humor," he said and then snorted with laughter at his little joke.

"Oh, I see. Go ahead and lock it. I would love that," she said and reached out and felt him up. He was rock hard and she was beginning to really get heated up. She had thought that they would talk first about Annie before they fucked but she just had to get a taste of that thing. It was definitely the biggest cock she had ever seen thus far.

After he locked the door, she was on him. She pulled his pants down and he was soon completely disrobed. He was definitely better looking without his clothes. He actually had a good body and because he was on the thin side that cock of his was the chief focal point. She got down on both knees and began sucking it even though she had a hard time getting her mouth completely on it.

"Oh, yeah," he said, putting his hands on her head. "That feels good."

His dick was so stiff. It was amazing that something that big could be that hard, but it was. She licked the head and slowly unbuttoned her shirt. He put a hand on one of her erect nipples and she felt electricity go through her body. She reached down to her clit and rubbed it a little with her other hand. She slipped her fingers down into her pussy and was realized that she was absolutely slippery. She finger-fucked herself a little as she continued to work his cock. When she tasted her fingers, he tensed up and she began to taste the precum. She stood up and took the rest of her clothes off.

"Do you want me to lick your pussy?" he asked with a big goofy grin.

"No, I'm past that. I want you to ram that big rod into me."

She leaned over the desk, moving papers out of the way and he entered her from behind. She was so wet and so hot that the size of him did not matter. He put his large cock into her easily and started fucking her hard. Her breasts swung as he fucked her and she came quickly.

"Fuck me, harder!" she said and he picked up the pace. That cock of his was just too much. It was a dream come true. He was a freak of nature and she was so happy that Julie had told her about him. She would remember this fucking for a long time. Her body convulsed over and over again with orgasm while he kept pounding her. A big dick like that was for power-fucking and he had the staying power to do it right.

"Let me turn you over," he said and she stood up and then lay back on his desk. She didn't care that she was lying on his papers, which from the look of them were student essays on some sort of boring historical subject. He obviously didn't care either because he was back inside her in an instant. She came again as he licked her tits while he fucked her drenched pussy. She was so slick at this point that a man with a lesser dick would have had to mop her off in order to stay inside her. However, he was big enough to maintain his traction.

Her eyes rolled back her head as he gave her the fucking of a lifetime. She had not had many men in her life. Yet. But she knew that it was going to be hard to top this one. After a while he pulled out and she eagerly got down on her knees took his load in her mouth. She had to gulp three times to swallow it. Wow, Julie had really been right about this one, she thought happily as she fingered herself to another orgasm.

After they had caught their breath, they sat in his office and talked about the Annie situation. Still nude, his semi-erection was a big distraction for her. Likewise was her hot body for him. It would probably be a very short conversation before they were at it again, but Alicia had come to find out a way to make Annie less uptight about sex. The fucking was just the bonus.

"I don't really know," he said. "I was really uptight, but Julie just came onto me and the next thing I know, I'm swinging and having sex with everybody. I mean, I'm a guy and guys are easy that way, but maybe that's the approach you should try with your friend."

"She's too uptight. Besides, girls are different. Julie says everybody wants to be this way, but finding a way to break her out of her shell is going to be tough."

The professor thought for a minute. "Why not let her watch a porno movie or something? That usually gets people horny. It always works at the swing parties, anyway."

Alicia thought about it for a minute. "I could leave one lying around and let her find it."

"Yes, that's a good idea. And maybe she might watch it when no one's looking."

Alicia thought about it. "It's worth a shot. I mean she's just so frigid. If I could get her drunk, it would be easy. But she won't even drink champagne. And that's what got me going. The champagne. After that I was ready to fuck the basketball team. But she just won't even have a taste. It's really not her fault though. Her mom has brainwashed her into thinking that one sip will make her into an alcoholic or something. That's her whole problem, her mother. She's afraid that if she doesn't do everything she says, her mom will disapprove of her."

"Wow, that is uptight," he added.

"If she could just get a taste of that big dick of yours, I think that would do it," she said eyeing his semi-hard penis. It was just laying there like a rolling pin. She could feel herself getting wet again and she knew that she was going to have to have another taste.

"But getting her to that point is the problem, though, right? I mean if she is so opposed to sex, how are you going to get her talked into fucking me?" he said, starting to stiffen. He was ready for Alicia again.

Alicia didn't answer however because she was already back on him and had his dick her mouth. And she had always been taught to not talk with her mouth full.

6

"It's like they were putting on a show for me, Alicia! It was disgusting!" Annie said on her cell phone as she walked to her car from her apartment. She was detailing the events that occurred when she had had her air conditioner fixed.

"Really?" Alicia said on the other side of the phone. "Do you think they....wanted you to join in?" she added hesitantly. She hoped so anyway. Just what she had already heard from Annie so far was enough to fuel several of her masturbatory fantasies.

"Duh. Of course. What would have been the point if they hadn't? I mean they were sucking and licking and going on.

Poor David had an..." She lowered her voice to a whisper. "...*erection*. But I don't blame him. He is just a guy after all. They can't control themselves the way that we can. He was just reacting to what was in front of him."

Alicia just sat there and listened. Why couldn't something like this have happened to her?

Annie continued. "I mean they've always wanted to turn me lesbian after all. Why else would they be doing what they were doing? "

Alicia could think of a lot of reasons, but didn't dare mention any of them. Annie still didn't know what she had been up to. In fact, all this talk about what was going on was making her extremely horny. She was thinking about her fucking at the hands of Professor Ricky and sex was completely dominating her mind. That and the idea of getting Annie into the real world and getting her fucked.

"Anyway, I'm going to Mom's. Do you want to meet me over there? We'll go over to the mall afterwards."

Alicia hesitated again. "I've got an errand to run first." She was planning on going to the adult bookstore and getting a DVD as Ricky had suggested.

Annie was getting a little tired of Alicia's newfound evasive weirdness so she just cut it short and didn't give her the chance to weasel out of it. "Good. I'll see you there," she said before Alicia could offer an alternative and then hung up.

Annie didn't really think much more about Alicia on the way over to her mother's. All she could think about was what the lesbians were doing and David's erection. It had been huge. He was a good looking guy, but that thing was just inappropriate. She just couldn't get the image of it out of her mind. His pants had been so tight she could see it perfectly through the fabric. She shook her head as if to shake these tempting thoughts from her head. She then began to think about what he had said about her being a fitness model. Doing this definitely improved her attitude and the thoughts of the lesbians and David's erection soon left the forefront of her mind. She was very honored at being asked but could understand why he had chosen her. She worked out a lot and had a good body so she didn't think it would be a bad thing for people to see the fruits of her labor. She might even be an inspiration for a lot of other women.

She pulled up to her mother's house and parked her Civic. It was the same house she had grown up in. It was a seventies-style rancher in one of the older residential areas of town. Annie's father had keeled over about ten years earlier due to his shock at the world not coming to an end when the clock struck midnight on Y2K. He had really been counting on a complete breakdown of society and was so pissed that he wasn't going to be able to start shooting everybody he didn't like that his high blood pressure had finally gotten the best on him. Annie's mother often wistfully thought that if he had only been able to hold out until 2012, his wishes for an apocalypse might just have come true.

Annie walked on into the house. Her mother was still dressed in a housecoat and watching TV. She was sitting on her floral printed couch with some inspirational literature on her lap. She seemed a little out of sorts like she had just been startled. On the TV was the *The Church of What's Happenin' Now with Brother Red Hair.* On the program, wild organ music was playing and Brother Red was running around and jumping and bringing the message which was one of free love and open minds.

"I hate that Brother Red Hair. He just makes TV preachers look so bad. Telling everybody that they can do just like they please."

"Well, you can turn the channel, Mom," Annie said and took the remote control.

Mom grabbed the remote back from her. "Don't turn that off. It reminds me of just how horrible this world has gotten." Then she turned her eyes down and pouted as to signify that she was once again disappointed in how far society had slid down the toilet.

Annie's mother was a good looking woman in her mid-forties. She had kept herself up, that was for sure. She had large breasts like Annie and still got ogled by a lot of men. She also had an absolutely smoking tanned body. Some people would have called her the ultimate MILF; however, they never dared to let her know they were thinking of her in this way because she was so intimidating in her piety.

Annie sat down and thought about telling her about what she had seen in the lesbians' apartment but decided not to. She realized that her mother was so pure of mind that such behavior would probably make her suffer the same fate as her father. She didn't want to be orphaned. She opted to tell her about David's suggestion that she start modeling instead.

"Fitness modeling? What's that?" her mother said suspiciously.

"It's modeling swimsuits and athletic wear. He said it because I'm in such good shape. It gives people who are trying to lose weight something to aspire to."

Her mother sighed judgmentally. "I don't know why people have to be so vulgar."

"But it's not like that, Mom," Annie protested. "David's a nice guy."

"It's still showing off your body. He was looking at you. When men look at you, it only means one thing. They want to use you."

"Mom!" she yelled. "You don't know what you're talking about."

"Oh, I know," she thundered. "You're the one who doesn't know what you're talking about! You need to remember your pledge! You're not even married yet and you're talking about having your pictures taken in a swimsuit!"

"So I have to get married to do that? Because it's not proper?" Annie was a little stumped. There was nothing in her pledge like that.

"Yes, you have to be married to do anything that gives you pleasure like that. After you're married, you can let your husband crawl on top of you and wiggle around until he gets done. And he can take pictures of you in a swimsuit if he still wants to look at you. But only *he* can look at them. You have to remember what it means when you say that you must cheerfully deny yourself pleasure."

"Yes," said Annie.

"That means *all* pleasure. Forever. Especially sexual pleasure. Even after you're married."

"I see," Annie said.

"Just listen to me and you'll be okay, Annie. You've really disappointed me in even bringing this up," she huffed.

Annie sat down and turned her attention to the TV. This just didn't sound right. Wasn't it enough that she didn't drink or smoke or really do much of anything? But all she was going to do was get her picture taken. And David was a friend. He surely didn't have any untoward motives. But then she thought about her pledge. Her mother was right. Probably.

A few minutes later, there was a knock at the door.

"Oh that's Alicia."

"Alicia," her mother muttered. "I've been hearing some things about her. I don't know if I want someone like her in this house."

"Why not?" Annie said puzzled.

"I heard she's been having the sex," her mother said. "I heard that she's a regular slut. She's been hanging out with that girl named Julie. The one who used to go to church with you."

"Really?" Annie said amazed. She couldn't believe it.

"I'm really disappointed that you're friends with someone like that. A common whore. "

Annie was stunned again. What was up with her mother? She could understand that she was upset about Alicia because they had been friends since grade school, but to talk about her like that? Especially since she really didn't know if it was true.

"Well, I'll have to ask her about it," Annie said and went to the door.

"Annie," her mother said as she got up. "Just take her outside. I don't want her in her. She's liable to bring a disease in here."

"Uh...okay," Annie said, not really knowing why her mother was being so mean.

"Well, see you later then," her mother said. "And remember what I told you about those swimsuits."

"Bye," Annie said and went out the door and met Alicia.

"You don't want me to come in?" Alicia asked, hoping that she didn't. She did not particularly want to see Annie's mother. She had just run her errand and was afraid that Annie's mother would be able to tell what she had been up to just by looking at her.

"Uh...no...I want to get going," Annie said, not really knowing what to say.

"Great," Annie said before she thought about it.

They got into Alicia's car. As they backed out of the driveway, Annie's mother stood at the window and watched them leave. After they were safely out of sight, she stood up and let her housecoat fall open. She was completely nude underneath it. Her body was completely tanned and very tight. She fished a joint out of her housecoat pocket and lit it up. Then she reached under the couch and pulled out a bottle of vodka and took a sip. She felt her nipples as they hardened up at the memory she had of fucking the Music

Director from church. She had really taught him a thing or two about playing the organ, she chuckled to herself.

She sat down and switched the TV over to the Hot Stuff Channel and rewound the DVR back to the place in the movie that she had been watching when Annie had so rudely interrupted her. A muscular female prison guard was dildoing a petite brunette with a night stick. She put her fingers to her pussy and gently rubbed her clit as she watched the action. She was wet again in no time. She put her fingers to her lips. She liked what she tasted.

Then she reached into the side table and pulled out a vibrator. She chuckled as she turned it on and applied it to her pussy. She watched the action on the screen and then felt that oh-so-familiar feeling take hold of her body as she came to orgasm. She took another toke and was now high as a kite. She thought about what she had said to Annie about her friend Alicia and the photo shoot and Cheerfully Chaste and then started cackling. These girls would find out how the world really worked one day. About how appearances were all that mattered and how people had to think of you in the *right way.* She realized that some people might look at her as some old hypocrite, but this is just the way things worked. Especially about sex. It was like the joke about Baptists that she had heard all her life. They're like cats when it comes to sex. Nobody ever sees them, but everybody knows they're doing it. This was her approach to almost everything in her life. Do what you want but act very pious about it. If people find out, then deal with it. No need in bringing on any judgment on yourself unnecessarily. She had always assumed that this was everybody else's philosophy as well.

She continued to sit there in a haze watching the movie for a little while longer then she suddenly looked at the clock on the mantle. She jumped up with a start. She was going to have to get ready. She had a date in a couple of hours. It was with a man she had met on the internet. He was only going to be in town for a little while. He was here to do something related to his wife's flower shop business.

Annie's mom looked in her closet for a minute trying to figure out what form-fitting and revealing outfit she would wear to the hotel where she was going to meet him. Then she rolled her eyes at herself for putting that much effort into it. She knew she shouldn't worry too much about what she was going to wear because she wouldn't be wearing it for long. It would be just like when the Music Director had come over. Clothing just had a way of getting in the way of fun. She cackled again and got ready.

7

Annie looked over at Alicia suspiciously as she drove to the mall. She wondered if it was true what her mother had said about her friend—that she had been slutting around all over town and doing all sorts of questionable things with all sorts of questionable people. She decided not to say anything. Her friendship with Julie had already been ruined because of Julie's extreme sexual behavior so she really didn't want to go there again. Especially so soon. Besides she was still a little upset at the way her mother had acted towards the idea of the photo shoot. She understood that a person had to display their piety at all times and always be quick to judge the shortcomings and sins of others, but it was just a few pictures. That was all. Her mother was just too old-fashioned.

Alicia sensed the tension in the car and nervously tried to make small talk.

"So how's your mom?"

"Good," Annie snapped.

She tried again with a few more innocuous questions only to achieve the same result. She eventually stopped trying.

She really didn't feel like talking anyway. She moved slightly on her seat. She was still a little sticky from what had happened to her on her errand just before she had come over to Julie's house. Of course she had been successful in her attempt to buy the adult DVD that Professor Ricky had suggested, however she had gotten a little more than that accomplished in the process. She had gotten gang-fucked as well. She knew that she probably still smelled of sex but hadn't really had time to clean up. She hoped that this was one time that Annie's naiveté in such matters would be a benefit.

It had all started innocently enough. Well, as innocently as a visit to the adult bookstore can go. She had driven out to the interstate to the Cinema Sexxx Adult Novelty and Bookstore and parked her Subaru. While she had always wanted to go to this place, she was still a little nervous about entering it. So naturally, after she had walked in, she was a little overwhelmed by all the sex toys and adult material. This place really seemed like home for her because it was all about sex. Even though it was run down with worn out carpeting and smelled slightly like mildew, she loved it. She was still a little turned on from the story Annie had told regarding the lesbians at her apartment complex so looking at all the sex stuff had made her pussy ache slightly with the need for cock. She just knew that she was going to have to buy one of those ten-inch jelly dongs.

She knew that she didn't have a lot of time because she had to meet Annie. Because of this she focused on finding something that she knew that Annie would respond to. While she knew that her friend was as uptight as they came, she knew that she always seemed fascinated by musclemen and black guys. Or at least she seemed to be. She knew that she had seen these types of magazines lying around Annie's apartment on several occasions. She also knew that Annie's boyfriend Jimmy was always reading them so it made sense that she might be interested in them as well. It was really the only information she had to go on so she figured that it would be as good a direction as any. As she perused the video racks and settled on a title for Annie—*Hood Rat White Ho Muscleman Gangbang 19*—she began to notice that all eyes were on her. The place was filled with trucker and biker types some of whom stank like diesel and motor oil. And body odor. She was a little flattered and knew that her short skirt and tight top were getting the response that she had hoped. Much to her friend Annie's chagrin, she had started dressing in a much more slutty fashion since she had been becoming more sexually active and had been very happy with the reaction that she always seemed to elicit in men and women. Some uptight people would look offended, but the stares and whistles and drool more than made up for any feelings of embarrassment she might have had.

After picking out the DVD she decided to check out. She walked to the counter. It was manned by a dirty looking biker-type with long hair and tattoos. His name tag read Buzz which seemed appropriate since he smelled like marijuana and his eyes were completely bloodshot. She sat the jelly dong and DVD on the counter

"Are you sure that dildo is big enough?" Buzz asked and laughed hoarsely.

Alicia turned red with embarrassment.

"Oh, it's all right. I understand. I know from personal experience that women like them big," he said and laughed again.

"The bigger the better," Alicia said, warming up to him a little and picking up on the fact that he was hinting that he had a big dick.

Buzz's penis started to rise at this.

"I'm going to have to stand up now," Buzz said and laughed. He did and moved his now hard penis over a little. "These jeans have a tendency to pinch it."

Alicia's eyes narrowed down on the imprint of his penis through his dirty looking Levis. It was almost down to his knee. "Why don't you let me see it?" she asked before she knew what she was saying.

"Here? I'm at work!" he said incredulously, leering.

"It's an adult bookstore," she said sarcastically, now fixated on his dick.

"Well, if you insist," he said and chuckled. He pulled down his pants and his erect member sprung up. He stroked it a little and Annie knew she was going to have to have it. It reached partially across the counter it was so huge. She put her hand out and stroked it a little. It was hot to the touch. Her mouth watered at the sight of it and her other hand went to her pussy. She had been horny when she had come in here and she was absolutely aching for it now. She leaned over and put her mouth on it and licked the tip. As with Professor Ricky, it was so huge that it was a little difficult for her to get her mouth on it, but because of her earlier experience she found a way and quickly had it deep in her mouth. She deepthroated a little of it, as much as she could at least and was so proud of herself that she became even wetter. It felt so good to her that her mouth so completely filled and could only imagine how her pussy would feel. It was going to be stretched out now for sure. Professor Ricky had found untouched territory in it with his massive dong, now she was going to have even more expansion.

After letting Alicia suck him for a few minutes, Buzz moved around to the other side of the counter. This gave Alicia a minute to get completely out of her clothes. She had such a gorgeous body, he thought. It was going to be real pleasure fucking her. Alicia didn't know it, but this sort of thing happened a lot in the bookstore. However, it was usually husbands bringing in their bored wives for a public fucking, so this was a little different—a single girl who was horny as hell coming in on her own. He was so happy that he worked here. The pay may have been shit, but the perks were outstanding.

He bent Alicia roughly over the counter and started licking her pussy. She moaned as his tongue went up and down her slit and became more and more turned on. She ground against his mouth and when he inserted three fingers into her vagina, she could wait no longer.

"Stick it in," she said breathlessly.

"I think I can handle that," he said and entered her slowly, making sure that she could handle his size. To his surprise she could. He began fucking her with a consistent rhythm, allowing her to get her groove on and start orgasming. Her tits rubbed against the counter as he pounded her into screaming orgasm after screaming orgasm.

Alicia was in heaven and her cries soon brought the attention of all the other customers. While Buzz continued to give her the fucking of a lifetime, there gathered an audience of bikers and truckers standing around watching the action and stroking their cocks. Watching them watching her only enhanced the experience for Alicia and she played up to the audience.

"But are you having a good time?" Buzz said as he continued to fuck her. She was just so wet now.

"Fuck yeah!" Alicia said and arched against him hard.

Soon, Buzz had had enough and blasted a line of jizz all over her ass. He rubbed it with his finger and put in her mouth. She hungrily ate it up and was still ready for more.

Still lying face first on the counter, Alicia caught her breath. Man, that was some fucking, she thought. But before she could turn around, he had another cock in her! All the guys who had been standing around watching her fuck were now going to take a turn! She came again just with the thought of it.

She didn't even turn around as one by one they fucked her. Each one pounding her hard and fast as they blasted their cum both into her and onto her. She lost count after the fourth one. She orgasmed so much that her legs grew weak as they had their way with her and satisfied their sexual desires. After a while, she was coated in jizz and was truly the happiest girl in the world.

After they were finished, she stood around in the nude talking for a while before she remembered that she had to meet Annie. She quickly dressed and grabbed her jelly dong and DVD and dashed out the door.

This is why she wasn't really bothered by Annie's bitchy behavior while they were in the car. She was just too blissed out. She had gotten fucked so much and so well lately that there was no way that she could be in a bad mood.

Soon the two girls made it to the mall and walked in.

"Where do you want to go first?" Alicia asked first.

"Let's go to Avenue 3. I've got some panties I need to take back. They're just too slutty," Annie said. She was still in turmoil about her mother and what she had said about Alicia. She was this close to saying something to her about it. She held her tongue though.

"Okay," Alicia said.

As the two girls made their way over to the clothing store, Avenue 3, they noticed a commotion going on at the food court. They walked over to see what was going on. Needless to say, they were surprised. A big muscular red-haired guy was there with his cronies having an impromptu wet t-shirt contest right there in the middle of the dining area. He and his buddies were shaking up soda pop and beer and spraying it on some girls. The girls were dancing to the muzak that was always playing at the food court. They didn't care one bit that they were interrupting people from eating their Chinese food, pizza slices and chicken sandwiches. In fact, they were almost defying anyone to say anything to them. Which, of course, no one would because the crowd was loving it.

"I think that's Cornbread Pritchett," Alicia said breathlessly, thinking about what the tree-trimmer had said about him.

"I just can't believe this!" Annie said ignoring her and getting angry. "I'm going to call mall security!"

"They're already over there," Alicia said pointing to a couple of guards. They were watching the proceedings from the side. They obviously weren't going to do anything about it. Their tongues were hanging out of their mouths as the girls took their shirts off and rubbed them all over Cornbread and his buddies. They pole danced around the kiddie rides, grinding against each other and dirty dancing.

"Shake it, baby! Shake it!" Cornbread hollered and sprayed them some more.

The girls then started suggestively slowly stripping out of their clothes.

Already horny from the afternoon, Alicia fought the temptation to go out and join them. These girls were hot and she could just feel her body against theirs. As she got a closer look, she realized that tree-trimmer had been telling the truth about Cornbread. She could clearly see the outline of his dick through his wet pants. He was hung and in a major way. She was strangely transfixed by him too. He was a real loudmouth and an oaf, but he was also sort of good looking in a Jethro Bodine sort of way. There was just something about him that turned her on. She knew that someday, somewhere, somehow, she would have to fuck him.

"This really makes me mad! How can they let something like this go on?" Annie complained.

"Well, his uncle owns the mall," Alicia said, crossing and uncrossing her legs and fighting the urge to rub her clit.

"I don't care. It's just not right. People acting like that."

Alicia didn't answer. Before she could stop herself, she absentmindedly put her hand to her breast and felt her hardening nipple.

Annie happened to be looking at her for a response and noticed her doing this. She was aghast. She couldn't take it anymore. "My mom was right about you! You are a slut now!"

"No, I'm not," Alicia said defensively, moving her hand away.

"Don't try to hide it. You've been acting weird for a while now. You just need to get out of the middle of the road and stop pretending that you're still staying true to the pledge. You need to just admit it. I'll still be your friend. I'll be disappointed in you, but I'll be your friend. I don't think we'll be able to talk for a while though."

"Well, thanks for the condescension," Alicia said a little miffed. How dare Annie talk to her like this! However, she was too turned on at the moment to think too much about it though. She would worry about it later.

"Let's leave," Annie said.

"I want to stay," Alicia said.

"We came in my car," Annie said, matter of factly. "I get to pick when we leave."

Reluctantly Alicia turned to leave with Annie but before they could leave, they heard a shout.

"Hey, Annie!"

They turned and looked.

"It's the two lesbians from the apartment complex. I thought they looked familiar. Those whores!" Annie said, fuming. They were the girls who were getting sprayed by Cornbread and his buddies.

"Watch this!" the lesbians said and started making out.

"Ugghhhh!" Annie screamed and ran. "I'm going crazy! I can't stand this!"

Alicia struggled to catch up with her as they made their way to the parking lot.

"I didn't even get to return those panties!" Annie said and pouted as they got into the car. Alicia didn't answer.

That was it for the conversation because Annie was so furious that she drove home without saying anything else. Alicia however, did manage to slip the DVD into Annie's pocketbook without her noticing.

After Annie dropped Alicia off at her car at her mother's house, she drove straight to her apartment so angry that she could barely see straight. She was glad that her mother wasn't home because she wasn't in the mood to see her again. She was also very disappointed and upset in Alicia.

Annie had a date over at Jimmy's apartment that night anyway. Hopefully, that would cheer her up. He was going to make a chocolate cake for them along with brewing massive quantities of sweet tea. Then they were going to go get ice cream. It was the typical sugar-based good time that they usually enjoyed. Sometimes she felt badly about indulging herself so much like that with Jimmy, but then figured since that was the only thing she was allowed to do, then she might as well go for it. Regardless, she still felt guilty about it afterwards.

After arriving home, she quickly jumped into the shower. Completely nude, the hot water ran over her body. She imagined that it was washing away all the filth that she had seen that day. If only it could have also washed her mind, she thought. She went over what had happened and the thought of Cornbread and his girls having such a good time right there in the mall just wouldn't leave her head. They were gyrating and rubbing all over each other. Then she thought about her friend Alicia's reaction. She thought about how she had been licking her lips and touching her breasts. She then thought about the lesbians and David's massive erection. It seemed like wherever she turned there were people having sex. Everything was about sex! She could feel her body start to heat up at this, but her Cheerfully Chaste training had taught her that now was the time to be strong and to keep her hands off her beautifully formed large breasts and to focus only on shaving her bikini line. She realized that she simply had to fight any impulse to put her fingers down *there*.

If she was honest with herself, she would have admitted that she was aching to have sex. It was a very powerful drive within her. Sometimes the urge would infect her dreams and she would have the wildest fantasies involving herself rubbing her body all over strange men and women. She was sure she had done that thing called orgasming in her sleep but had never told anyone. Certainly not her mother. Or Alicia either. She didn't want anyone to think badly of her.

No, she knew she was normal. She was just good. She was chaste and she always did what was right. However, as she had gotten older and moved into her early twenties she felt that her desire to have sex and to be sexual was getting to be overwhelming. Sometimes she felt like she was going to explode and the sexual acts she had been seeing lately had been almost overwhelming. She had actually found herself almost drooling today when she had watched the girls dancing with Cornbread. This is the main reason why she had gotten so angry. She was disappointed in herself.

Still, she couldn't believe that Alicia of all people had let her down. First her mentor, Julie, and then her best friend? How was she going to be able to stay strong now? Especially when the temptation was so strong? She really was the last one holding out and doing the right thing.

She moved the washcloth over her body and it was almost too much to keep it from lingering on her breasts. She found herself actually wanting to put her nipple in her mouth. She wanted to start sucking it. It would be so easy because her breasts were so large.

She then shook her head angrily. She was disgusted with herself for having such a thought. What was going on with her? Everything was just so confusing.

She quickly finished her shower before she did something she was going to regret and put on her clothes and grabbed her purse.

As she was walking out, she noticed the DVD sticking out of it.

"This must be Alicia's," she said as she looked it over. "*Hood Rat White Ho Muscleman Gangbang 19*," she murmured. It did look good, she thought, looking at the pictures of the muscular black men on the front of it. She was reminded again of David and the pictures of Harold Hercules and other black men in Jimmy's magazine. The feelings of warmth came over her again. She realized that she actually aching with desire.

Then, almost automatically she came to her senses again. "What filth!"

She turned her nose up almost derisively at it.

"I must cheerfully deny myself pleasure," she said to herself and with an almost herculean effort put the DVD down. "I'll throw this trash out later," she said. Then she left her apartment as quickly as possible.

After retrieving her car from Annie's mother's place, Alicia drove home. She felt really bad about what had happened at the mall. Not necessarily because of the sex, because she had really wanted to participate in that, but because of the way that Annie had spoken to her. She knew that she had disappointed Annie and that had hurt her. This didn't change the fact that her friend was wrong, but Alicia could empathize because she had once been brainwashed that way as well. If she could just break through to her, then everything would be so much easier.

She sat down on her couch. She attempted to clear her mind by watching TV, but soon inevitably found her hand going between her legs. She pulled off her skirt and panties and absentmindedly rubbed her clit while she watched a program about a banker who had tried to force his wife into a sex change. It was just so weirdly fascinating that she couldn't help but watch. The feel of her shaved pussy was always a comfort to her when she was stressed, or any other time for that matter.

This was something she often did this when she watched TV nowadays. Since she had started having recreational sex, she would masturbate absentmindedly, almost bringing herself to orgasm and then backing off. Usually, she would finish herself off eventually and the pleasure would be absolutely exquisite. She was also planning on breaking in the ten-inch jelly dong that she had bought at the adult bookstore. She already had it sitting on the coffee table ready for use. The feeling of Buzz's enormous cock was still in her mind and she was hoping the ten-incher would come close to replicating the feeling of fullness she had experienced with him. She wasn't able to stick with her hand for long, though because the more she thought about that big dong, the more she knew she was going to have to have it inside her. She licked the end of it to it get a little wet and then slowly inserted it. It felt great. She stroked it in and out and in and out, each thrust bringing herself closer to orgasm. It wasn't long before all the built up orgasms exploded into one. It was pure heaven for her. She sat there for a second savoring the feelings of satisfaction and then fell asleep.

She still had jelly dong inside her when she awoke with a start and looked at the clock. She had been asleep for a couple of hours. For some reason, the brief amount of sleep had given her a new clarity on the situation with Annie. She knew that she had taking the wrong approach by hiding what she was doing. She should have been more open about it. She might have even gotten Annie to listen to her side of things if she had just come out with it. After all they had been friends since childhood. Being sexual didn't change who she was as a person after all.

She took the dildo out, got dressed and left her apartment. She got into her Subaru and drove over to Annie's place.

Alicia couldn't wait to talk to her friend. She knew that if she was just honest with her and told her about all she was missing and how Cheerfully Chaste wasn't necessarily such a good thing and how much better she would feel about life if she would just loosen up, then Annie would understand. She just had to be brave. She just had to take a chance.

Screwing up her courage, she walked from the parking lot to Annie's apartment and knocked on the door few times but no one answered.

She waited for a few minutes, but then the door to the next apartment opened.

"Annie's not home." It was Sunny, one of the girls that Alicia seen earlier at the mall with Cornbread. She was drinking from a tallboy can of beer.

"Do you know when she will be back?" Alicia asked.

"How should I know? She doesn't tell us anything," April, the other girl, said as she walked up behind Sunny. "She's probably with that weird boyfriend of hers drinking sweet tea, but I wouldn't know for sure."

"She thinks we're degenerates," Sunny laughed.

Alicia gulped. These girls were beautiful and the thought of them nude and gyrating at the mall was still on her mind. They were both wearing short-shorts and tight cut off t-shirts which barely covered up their big breasts. Their stomachs were tight and tan and Alicia could not stop staring at them.

"I know, she's said that before," Alicia said.

"Do you want to come in and wait for her?" April said and winked at her. "Or are you like Annie and scared that you might like us?"

"Yeah, are you uptight like your friend?" Sunny said and ran her fingers down Alicia's arm.

"I'll think you'll find that I'm nothing like Annie," Alicia said and moved in close to Sunny.

"That's what we thought," April said and laughed and put her hand on Alicia's breast.

The three women went inside the apartment and closed the door. They couldn't get to the bedroom fast enough and left a trail of clothes behind them as they lustily went at each other. They were grabbing and man-handling each other like they were a bunch of men pawing a hot wife at a group grope. This was nothing like how Alicia ever imagined this kind of situation would be like. She thought that sex with lesbians would be softer and more relaxed. However, these girls were rough. She loved it.

The three of them toppled onto the bed in a sex-fueled frenzy. In an instant, April was sucking Alicia's clit and Sunny was licking her tits. Alicia's body was being overloaded with sensations and it almost felt like the two women were going to devour her. There were hands and tongues and pussies all over her. She would never have even been able to imagine an experience so wonderfully exhilarating. April brought her to a bucking orgasm quickly but she still wasn't finished with her. She could see April licking and sucking even harder as she played with herself. Sunny soon climbed on her face and she eagerly gave the bleach blonde cunnilingus, licking her slit and sticking her tongue into her engorged vagina as she rode her chin. She tasted great. Like sex. Soon she worked her to a froth as the woman rubbed her pussy against her mouth. This thought alone made her cum again.

Group sex with women was great and Alicia was glad that she had added it to her growing list of sexual experiences. They continued on like this for a while and eventually Sunny and April switched out, still leaving Alicia as the focus of their attention. April rode Alicia's face to an explosive orgasm and Alicia had a couple of more.

"Let's try something else," April said with a wicked little laugh. "Get up on all fours," she said to Alicia who obeyed without thinking. What was happening was great so she had no reason to question anything they were doing.

After she was up on all fours, and just when Alicia had thought that things couldn't get any better, Sunny put on a strap-on. A big strap-on. She got behind Alicia and entered her roughly. Alicia was ready for it, especially after the ten inch dong and the earlier fucking by Buzz. She thrust herself lustily against the strap-on which intensified the feelings of pleasure felt by Sunny on the other side of it. It worked against her pussy and had to bite her lip to keep from cumming too soon.

But then out of nowhere, Alicia felt a slap on her ass. Then another.

"Ouch!" She said and turned around. April was spanking her. With a ping-pong paddle!

"Just turn around and take it," April said. "You'll love it."

Sunny thrust even harder and every time she went out, April spanked her. They built up a rhythm to this and pretty soon Alicia couldn't stop from cumming. The heat from the paddle was counterbalanced by the pleasure of the insertion. It was an overload of sensations and it wasn't long before she was weak in the knees from orgasm. She collapsed on the bed and watched as April and Sunny scissored their vaginas together and began humping hard as they finished each other off.

Afterwards they sat around the bed drinking tallboys and laughing. Alicia got up to get herself another one. This had been one of the best experiences of her life. She had had sex with a few girls before but nothing on a par like this. These girls, being lesbians, were pros. They definitely knew their way around a woman.

"So, if you're like this? What's the deal with Annie?" Sunny said

"Oh, yeah, Annie," Alicia said. She had cum so much she had almost forgotten why she had come over. She briefly explained about Annie which seemed to turn on the girls even more.

"Wow," Sunny said. "I didn't know that's why she was so uptight." She paused for a second. "She's just so hot. It's such a waste that she's such a prude."

"I know," Alicia said.

"Well, enough about her. Let's talk about you," April said. "Cornbread is having a party over at his place on Saturday night. You ought to come."

"Really?" she said. "I've heard he has some great parties."

"I'll bet you have," Sunny said and smiled. With that, the sex started again.

10

Later that night at Jimmy's place, Annie was still reeling from the events that had just transpired. She couldn't believe what she had just done. She just couldn't believe that she had turned this corner. She was so ashamed and embarrassed. Yet, at the same time, however, she was overjoyed and relieved. She had finally given in to temptation. She had just had sex with Jimmy. She had broken her pledge. She wanted to hide. She wanted to run. She wanted to fuck.

"Wow! That was great," Jimmy said still a little stunned. He had been looking at one of his muscle magazines when he noticed that Annie was looking over his shoulder. He had been especially interested in this photo spread of Harold Hercules. Harold was one of his favorites and was a gigantic black body-builder. The guy was built. The photo-spread was so good and so in-your-face that Annie couldn't help but notice it as she brought Jimmy yet another glass of sweet tea. But it wasn't Harold's muscles that she noticed. It was his bulge. It was huge! That, along with his muscles, was enough to make her stop what she was doing and stare.

"He is so big," Annie said breathlessly, her mouth beginning to water and her body starting to tingle. All those years of abstinence had made her have a hair trigger when it came to sex. Sometimes, she felt like she was going to explode. Somehow or another, her pledge had always kept her in check, but this time was different. It was like her sexual tension had built up to a point that it could not be contained and when she leaned over Jimmy to get a better look, the sensation of her breasts touching his shoulder was too much. The dam was on the verge of breaking. She thought about all the sex she had been exposed to lately. She thought about the lesbians and David's gigantic erection. She thought about Alicia getting so turned on at the mall. She looked down and saw the imprint of Jimmy's large penis through his jeans and that was it. She went into a lust-filled daze and in a second she was all over him. The idea of denying herself pleasure was finally being overruled.

Jimmy was surprised but glad when Annie decided to jump his bones. He had had sex before but it had been an awkward situation with a girl in his school chorus back when he was in high school. He hadn't really known what he was doing and she hadn't either. As a result, their attempt at sex had resembled something out of a comedy routine rather than a hot encounter. He never got another chance to show her what he was capable of because afterwards she had changed schools. Jimmy's friends said that this was because he was horrible at sex but he figured that maybe it was just a coincidence that she had moved. At least that's how Jimmy reassured himself. That's one reason why when it came to Annie, just having her on his arm was enough for him. She was beautiful and it made him look good to have her with him. He didn't want her to move away from him either. Regardless, he was overjoyed when she grabbed his already erect member.

"Why, you're huge," Annie said amazed as she fished his johnson out of his pants. He was. To be such a skinny guy, Jimmy had a massive dick. It hadn't had much action, but it truly was a thing that would make a girl's mouth water. Annie had always suspected he was hung from the way his pants would tent sometimes when he was sleepy and reading muscle magazines, but she really didn't know enough about such things to be sure. All she knew that it made her tingle inside to think about it.

She began by sucking his dick, all the while feeling herself heat up. She really wasn't sure how to approach it because up until now, the only activity she and Jimmy had engaged in was the occasional peck on the cheek but she started out by working the head. He didn't complain so she was sure she was doing it right. All she knew was that her pussy was drenched and she knew that she was going to orgasm soon. Along with the feelings she had from some of the sexy dreams she had had, she had read enough literature from the Cheerfully Chaste program to know about a body's reaction to sexual stimulus. Her pledge was far from her mind because the feeling of the building orgasm felt so good that she wanted it more than she wanted anything else. She moved closer to Jimmy's knee and hunched it reflexively. It was just so natural she thought and then her body began to convulse and felt bliss that she had never felt before. She also felt a little ashamed too but these feelings were soon overtaken by the feelings of another wave of sexual current. The thoughts of denying herself pleasure were there, but somehow it was not so easy to say it right now. And if she did, there would be nothing cheerful about it. Besides she was tired of denying herself pleasure. Just this one time wouldn't hurt.

Jimmy of course was feeling elated. Annie sucking his cock was something he had dreamed about but never thought would happen. He felt like he was going to blow from the start. When she started humping his knee while she worked his cock, he thought she was going to lose it.

"Let me fuck you," he said eagerly, hoping that she didn't change her mind.

Annie readily complied and lay back on the couch. Any feelings of embarrassment or shame had left her. She would have burned all her Cheerfully Chaste certificates at this time just to feel his massive cock inside of her. She had already had another orgasm and wanted more. She felt alive for the first time ever. She felt like an adult. She felt like an animal. She wanted sex and she wanted it now!

Jimmy put her on her back and, even though he was fairly inexperienced, he knew enough where to put his gigantic dong. He pulled her panties off and lifted her skirt. She had already unbuttoned her shirt and her enormous tits were on display. They were so round. She was breathing slightly harder than usual so they were heaving up and down. Jimmy loved this and began to suck and bite at the nipples. Annie moaned at his effort. As the feelings of pleasure coursed through her body, she wondered how she could have allowed herself to miss out on such experiences. Now, she understood all about Julie and why she had taken her particular route.

"Stick it in," Annie said breathlessly.

Jimmy did not need any more encouragement than that and immediately but slowly put his big member inside and began to gently fuck her.

"There like that," she said, unable to believe just how good his penis felt inside of her. "Keep doing that," she said breathlessly as she moved against him and worked towards another climax. But then, all of a sudden, he groaned and his eyes rolled back in his head. He had orgasmed. Prematurely.

"Oh, no!" Annie said and hit him. "You can't cum so soon!"

"I'm sorry," he said. "You're just so hot I couldn't control myself."

"Thank you, I think," she said huffily, "I just wanted my first time to be a little more spectacular than that."

"We can try again later," he said pleadingly.

"I think we'll have to."

That had been a half-hour ago. Now the reality of what she had done was settling in. Annie, the keeper of the pledge, the person who had sat in judgment of all things sexual had let herself succumb to the pleasures of the body. She allowed herself to do the one thing that she had prided herself on not doing. She had fucked her boyfriend. And while mildly ashamed, she was also very proud of herself. She got it. She understood now. While she had built sex up to be this very big terrible thing and this very hard and fast line that could not be crossed, in reality it hadn't been like that. It had been very natural and not really that big of a deal. It had been fun and it had felt good. The orgasms also felt like something that should have been a part of life along time ago. She was ready for more.

But there was a problem.

What would everybody think about her now? She began to panic at this thought. People would call her a hypocrite. They would make fun of her. They would laugh at her. She was going to have to keep this to herself. She was going to have to hide it. She had cultivated an image of purity and of abstinence. How would it look if she would were to come out as someone who had had sex? It would ruin her.

But then her thoughts were suddenly interrupted by a more pressing matter.

"I'm ready if you are," Jimmy said and pointed to his enormous woody. "I'll try to do better next time."

Just the sight of it made Annie wet again. I am such a slut now, she thought realizing that she was not going to say no. "I'm ready, too," she said. "But you better not say anything about this to anybody, you hear?" she said with just the slightest bit of threat in her voice. "That is if you want to keep doing this."

"Sure thing," Jimmy gulped.

With that she pounced on him again and while he did a much better job fucking her and gave her a couple of orgasms, he was not able to completely satisfy her and came before she was completely finished. But then again, there was no chance that she was going to be finished anytime soon. All those years of saving herself had built up a hunger for sex that was apparently insatiable.

She groaned. Jimmy was just not going to be able to keep up with her.

"We can try again," he said helplessly. "I thought I did better that time."

Annie agreed but wondered if all men came as easily as Jimmy? He was spent and she was barely starting. This was a problem that she was going to have to think about. It was too bad that she couldn't talk to Julie or anyone else about it. They would never stop laughing at her. She had too much of an image to uphold. They would never let her live it down. And they probably would never accept her as one of their own because of all the stuff she had said about girls like them. She would have to do the research on her own.

Then she remembered the DVD that Alicia had left in her car.

11

Annie sat glassy-eyed staring at the TV screen. It was the next day and she had called into work sick. She had been awake since early that morning and had been masturbating to the porn video that Alicia had left in her purse since she had gotten up. She hadn't even bothered to put on any clothes. She just sat on the couch in the nude with the remote control in her hand, rewinding and fast-forwarding to all the parts that especially turned her on. This was pretty much the whole movie. She was transfixed. She just could not get enough. It was like fucking Jimmy the night before had unlocked something and watching the DVD only made it more unlocked. She could not take her eyes off the muscular black men and tight-bodied white chicks on the TV. She ached to have cock in her and to lick pussy. A part of her had been opened up. It was like a door had been opened that could not be shut. Each orgasm she had took her further and further away from the delusions that she had been under while attending Cheerfully Chaste. Also she couldn't help but notice how these guys seemed to last much longer and fuck much harder than Jimmy. Of course, they were professionals, but it was a pretty big difference and only made her mind reel with the possibilities.

"I just didn't know what I was missing," she said to herself as a hot brunette wrapped her lips around the nine-inch cock of a bandana wearing gangbanger. She thought about what her mother had always told her about alcohol. "One drink and you're ruined," Annie realized the same thing was true about cock. "One cock and you're ruined," her mother should have said. Except, in this case, she liked being ruined. She knew that she had to have more cock. A lot more cock.

At first, she had wanted to call Alicia and tell her all about her revelation and how she understood the life-changing qualities of good sex. She wanted to embrace her friend and tell her how sorry she was for the things she had said. But then her rigid upbringing kicked in. She thought about church and Cheerfully Chaste. She couldn't let anyone know about this. What would they think? Especially after everything she had said about slutty girls and people with loose morals. They would laugh at her. They would mock her. She would have to keep her mouth shut about this. No one must know. At least no one she knew or who knew her.

She watched the TV and masturbated some more, but suddenly she heard a knock on the door.

"Annie? You home?" came the voice on the other side of the door. It was David. "I came to check on your air conditioner. I wanted to see if it's still working okay."

Annie's heart leapt. It was like a genie had granted her wish and sent her what at that moment she was most desiring. She realized that she simply *had* to have to have sex with David. She also now realized what the feelings she had always had about him meant. She had been lusting for him. She had always liked being around him and looking at his body, but now she knew that she was going to have to fuck him.

"I'm coming," she said not bothering to put on any clothes or turn off the porn DVD. She wanted there to be no misunderstandings about her intentions.

David was so stunned at what he saw that he couldn't say anything when she opened the door. At first he wanted to run because didn't want to lose his job again like he had at the other apartment complex, but when she grabbed his hand and pulled him into the apartment, he knew everything was going to be all right.

"I've been wanting to see what's under these clothes for a long time," Annie said and started undressing him.

Within seconds David was completely nude. Annie almost gasped at the sight of him. He was muscular and his large penis was quickly moving from semi to fully erect. Annie couldn't believe the muscles. For someone who was known for always trying to get out of working, he was ripped.

She was down on her knees in front of him immediately, worshipping his cock. She couldn't believe that she was even doing this. It was so unlike her. But still she was pleased. It was a dream come true, especially after watching the DVD. It was like the movie was coming to life. She had come so far in the past few hours.

David couldn't believe his good luck either as he watched Annie go up and down on his dick. It felt good and though she was a little inexperienced at giving head, she knew enough to get the job done. He would have to teach her a little bit more about how to properly work his cock, but there would be plenty of time for that in the future. This was because he knew that she would want to do this again. They always did. He also knew that she still had almost a year left on her lease. What she was doing was good enough for now and still felt great.

As he looked at her sucking him off, he realized that her big boobs were so ripe and inviting that he simply was going to have to tit-fuck her. He had fantasized about doing this ever since he had first seen her. He led her over, her mouth still on his dick to a chair and he sat down. Then he pulled her up a little bit and put his cock between her breasts. Instinctively, she knew what she was supposed to do and she moved up and down his shaft, occasionally licking the precum that was now coming up on the end of his dick. She loved the feeling of his big cock between her large breasts and was happy that he introduced this sexual act to her.

After a little bit of that, David was ready to have a taste of her pussy so he positioned her on the couch and buried his mouth between her legs. She tasted like sex from all her masturbation that morning and his cock ached to enter her. Still he licked and sucked. She arched against his mouth and came immediately with a loud groan.

"You've got to stick that black cock inside me," she gasped as he licked. This is what she had been waiting for and couldn't wait to feel him inside her.

He put her over on her stomach and entered her doggie style. He entered her slowly and soon was completely in. She thrust against him and the friction of her clit touching his balls was enough to send her into orgasm again. He couldn't hold back now and he really started fucking her. He might have been less than enthusiastic when it came to working, but fucking was another story entirely. He picked up speed and started putting her through her paces. Ramming her and pushing his big cock further and further into her. In and out. In and out. Her big breasts swung and she couldn't resist licking her nipples while he gave it to her. It was the most exquisite thing she had ever felt. This was the way it must feel like to be fucked properly, she thought remembering her experience with Jimmy the night before. He had tried his best but it was nothing like this. David knew what he was doing and he was doing it right. She was truly worked up to a froth and she couldn't help but cum with a massive shudder as he continued to pound her.

At her last orgasm, David couldn't hold back. She was just too damned sexy and he pumped her a few more times and pulled out. She eagerly put his cock in his mouth and he coated the back of her mouth. He had still had a little bit more left and ejaculated what was left on to her boobs.

Annie was so happy but kind of scared of what she was doing. This was completely new territory for her but she liked the look of the neighborhood. If there had been any doubt about this change in attitude since she had fucked Jimmy, she didn't have it now. She could definitely understand why Julie and Alicia had turned their backs on Cheerfully Chaste.

But then she thought about Jimmy. What was she going to do about him? He was her boyfriend after all. She just hadn't been able to control herself when David had knocked. It was like her lust was more powerful than any ideas of monogamy she had for Jimmy. What was she going to do? She decided that she wouldn't tell him about it. This part of her life was going to have to stay secret. As long as she kept fucking him, he probably wouldn't care. Besides fucking David on the side would probably help her help him. She could learn more about sex and in turn teach Jimmy. And remembering the previous night made her realize that he probably needed all the help he could get.

David stood there for a minute, his still wet cock semi-hard, admiring Annie's full ripe breasts and tight stomach. He took a breath.

"So, I see your air conditioner is working," he said for lack of a better thing to say. After the initial lust had been sated, he realized that they didn't have much to talk about.

"You fixed it," Annie said licking her lips and feeling herself growing wet again. David just had such an amazing body, she just didn't want to take her hands off him.

David paused for a second trying to think of something else to say. "So what about that photo shoot? You think you want to do it?"

"I'm up for anything you want me to be," she said and reached out and started stroking his dick. It stiffened immediately at her touch. She was ready for more.

12

A few days later, Alicia wondered exactly what she was going to do about Annie. She had dropped the DVD off but had no idea if Annie had gotten the hint. She wondered if the DVD had awakened anything in her friend that might have been lying dormant. She wanted to call her but was still a little afraid to after the things Annie had said at the mall. She felt that Annie was still angry with her otherwise she would have called her by now. It was very unlike them to go without talking for so long unless something was wrong.

"It's that mother of hers," Alicia said to herself a little testily as she got dressed. "She's just brainwashed her." Whenever she thought about Annie's mother, she always found herself getting a little angry. Not only had Annie's mother's piousness affected Annie, but it had also affected her too. Sometimes, before she had "given in to temptation," and started having sex, she would think sexual thoughts and want to masturbate but would stop at the thought of Annie's mother's scolding voice. While a little on the strict side, her own parents had always been more relaxed than Annie's mother. She couldn't believe that she had been suckered in. The fact that equally disturbed her now that she was seeing things in a more sexual light was the fact that Annie's mother was so hot. If she had been some frumpy old thing, it would have made more sense. But she had a smoking body and big boobs! She still wore skirts and long hair unlike the other short haired women of her age around town. All the other women her age had seemed to have just given up and were styling themselves purely for comfort and ease of maintenance. However, Annie's mom was a real babe. It just didn't make sense.

"It's just not right, her being like that," Alicia said. "It's such a waste."

Annie continued to mull over the situation and walked out of her apartment and went to her car. She decided that a day of shopping at the mall was exactly what was needed to help clear her head. She felt a little bad because she usually always went shopping with Annie, but the thought that she was finally dressing the way she wanted made the ache of doing it alone a lot easier to bear. She was so happy to finally be able to wear a short skirt and no panties without Annie pointing a judgmental finger at her. The air blowing up her skirt onto her smooth, shaved pussy felt great. She was also wearing a very revealing top that showed a lot of cleavage. She realized that she probably looked more like a stripper than anything, but she didn't really care. It just felt good to finally be herself.

After she arrived to the mall, she decided to go in at the food court entrance. The brief walkway that led up to it was lined with trees and littered with cigarette butts and beer bottles. As she walked, she noticed two very well-built guys in hardhats standing around smoking cigarettes. There were chainsaws and pruners lying on the sidewalk beside them. The men were dirty from working, but they still looked very hot in their wife-beater t-shirts and jeans. Their muscular tattooed arms glistened with sweat. They also looked vaguely familiar.

"Hey, girl!" one of them said. "That outfit is hot!"

Then she realized who it was. It was the tree trimmers from Julie's place. She felt a sexual tingle as she recognized them.

"Hey, guys."

"Why don't you come over to the truck and let us get a better look at that outfit," the other one said and licked his lips.

She knew where this was going and bit her lip at the memory of their large cocks and muscled bodies.

Their truck was parked right next to where they were working.

"I think you'll like it," she said and walked over to the truck. The tree trimmers slapped her on the ass.

On the other side of the truck one of the tree trimmers got behind her while the other stayed in front of her as they looked her over and moved in close. The one behind her put his hand between her legs, rubbing her shaved pussy.

"Mmmm…no panties. I love that. Easy access."

"That's the point," she murmured getting wet at his touch.

The other one leaned in and kissed her neck and then got down on his knees and started licking her clit. The other one started kissing her from behind and put his hand under her shirt, rubbing her hard, erect nipples.

Alicia grabbed the head of the one who was licking her and pulled him into her, and ground into his face. He licked even harder and soon she was dripping. The other one pulled her skirt up behind her and unzipped his pants and put his thick cock behind her, rubbing up against her.

Soon she couldn't handle it anymore and pushed the guy's face away from her pussy. He stood up and she quickly unzipped his pants and bent over and began sucking his cock. Correctly reading the signal that she was giving, the one behind her dropped his jeans and entered her pussy. Even though he had a sizable thick cock, he entered her easily and began fucking her.

In front of her, she sucked the other one's heavy cock, barely able to deepthroat him. Still she managed and the sensation of the penis in her mouth and the other one in her pussy was too much and she began to orgasm. She whimpered a little bit and then took a look around her. In her haste to be fucked, she had assumed that when they had gone to the other side of the truck they would be out of the full view of anyone who was passing by. She was wrong.

They were even more exposed because the other side of the truck was in full view of the other side of the parking lot and the outdoor portion of the food court. It was usually empty due to the extreme heat during this time of the summer, however it was now it was filled with people watching them. She could see that they had attracted quite an audience. Including the lesbians and Cornbread Pritchett who was hooting and hollering and taking pictures with his camera phone.

"Get it girl!" he whooped and hollered and high-fived his buddies.

There were probably fifty to a hundred people watching her fuck the tree trimmers. This turned her on even more. Even mall security was there watching her with open mouths massaging their cocks. She knew that she was quite a sight with her skirt up and her tits hanging out of her top. She knew that if she had been watching herself, she certainly would have been masturbating as well.

She picked up the pace and thrust even harder against the one behind her and sucked the big rod of the other one, quickly bringing up the precum. She licked her lips as she tasted it.

"Now, switch," she said.

The cock that she had been sucking was even thicker and heavier than the other one. It filled up and stretched her pussy. She took the one in front of her up to the hilt in her mouth and his eyes almost rolled back in his head as she turned on the suction.

She was ready for another orgasm and was soon writhing against the other one. She took a look at her audience which caused her climax to come quickly. The precum came again and this time she knew that he wasn't going to be able to hold it, not with the fucking she had already given him. Her blowjob was too much for him. She clamped down on his cock and he blasted into her throat. She didn't lose a drop.

She continued to grind against the thick cock of the other one until she felt him tense up. He was going to cum; she bucked against him and squeaked out one more orgasm before he blasted all over her ass.

After they finished, the crowd started clapping. Red-faced but happy, she took a bow. Now that the entertainment was over, the crowd dispersed back into the air-conditioned comfort of the mall.

She said goodbye to the tree trimmers and walked towards the mall. Cornbread motioned her over to where they were sitting.

"This is the one we told you about, Cornbread," April said, giving her a wink.

"I can shore see you were right about her," Cornbread said and licked his lips. The woody he had grown during Alicia's fucking was still quite prominent and could easily be seen through his pants. Especially since he was making no attempt to hide it.

"This girl is insatiable," Sunny said.

"Thanks," Alicia said. Even though she had been fucked very seriously by the two tree trimmers, Cornbread's hard-on was making her wet again.

Cornbread leaned in towards her. He was awash in Polo cologne. "Do you want to break you off a piece of ol' Cornbread?" he asked, leering.

"It depends on what you're talking about," Alicia said.

"What's that supposed to mean?" Cornbread asked. Due to his money and car, his pick-up attempts usually worked like a charm.

"Well, if you're talking about actual cornbread, then no. I don't eat carbs. But if you're talking about that big cock I can see through your pants, then I'm definitely up for that."

At that Cornbread started howling and heehawing with laughter. "You're definitely going to have to come to my party then! A girl like you is just what we need!"

Alicia smiled, but then she noticed something, or rather someone, out of the corner of her eye. It was Annie and she was walking towards them. She looked as if she was in her own little world because she didn't even act as though she even recognized Alicia. Unknown to Alicia, the fact of the matter was that she was in her own little world because she had just been to Elizabeth's Misadventure, the lingerie store. She had gone there to buy some sexy underwear for David. And Jimmy. She had managed to find a see-thru thong and undersized bra. She was so horny she could barely think straight and couldn't wait to get back home and model the outfit for David or Jimmy. Whoever was home. She hoped David, but Jimmy would do. She could always show him a few things that she had learned from David if it came to it.

"Annie!" Alicia said and waved as Annie approached.

At this, Annie stopped. Then she saw Alicia. And the lesbians. And Cornbread and his buddies. Reflexively she put the Elizabeth's Misadventure bag behind her. She couldn't let these people know what she had been up to. What if they could read her mind? What if the fucking she had had over the last few days had changed her appearance? What if they could tell that she was no longer a virgin? What would they think of her? They would all start laughing if they knew.

"Alicia," she said. Then, before she realized what she was doing, she started in on her friend. "I see that the sexual deviants have decided to let you hang out with them."

"It's not like that, Annie," Alicia protested. "We really need to talk about some things. I think I can help you."

"You can't help anyone. You're just a slut. You open your legs for everyone. You're just trashy."

At this Cornbread started laughing. "You going to let that stuck up little piece of ass talk to you like that?"

"She's my friend. Don't talk to her like that," Alicia said. "I'm trying to help her get over this."

Annie rolled her eyes. "I don't need *your* help doing anything."

"I'm sorry then," Cornbread said. "But I think the only thing that's going to help this girl is a good hard fucking."

At this, Annie turned red.

"Cornbread! Don't talk to her like that!" Alicia angrily said to him.

Cornbread just started laughing. He patted his hard-on and winked at Annie. "She knows I'm right."

"Annie, I'm sorry." Alicia said.

Annie looked at Cornbread's massive erection and then ran off without saying anything. Once she got to her car, she started laughing. She had so wanted to tell them what was what and to get down on her knees and show Cornbread a thing or two, but she realized that she had done the right thing. Besides, with Alicia there she couldn't have done anything anyway. Alicia would have just judged her. She chuckled again. Cornbread was right but not in the way that he thought. The only thing that was going to help her at the moment *was* a good hard fucking. That's why she was going to find David and get one.

13

Walking around the workout facility Annie never felt sexier. It was the day of the photo shoot and the photographer had rented the place out for their exclusive use. It was just going to be the photographer and the other models that would be there. She was wearing stilettos and a micro-sling bikini that barely covered up anything. It had been provided by whoever was sponsoring the shoot and essentially consisted of two ribbons that barely covered her nipples and met between her legs so that it just covered her freshly shaved pussy. She had decided to go completely bare down there because she had no idea just how skimpy the swimsuits were going to be. It felt so sexy too and she knew that this was definitely going to be her new look. In addition to her and David there were two other models there. One of them was a heavily muscled, tanned surfer-dude like blonde guy and the other was a female bodybuilder who was super hot. She wore a micro-sling bikini as well. Annie figured that this was probably going to be a theme in the shoot.

She walked over to David who was oiling himself up for the photo shoot. His muscles glistened and his bulge was barely contained by his banana hammock. The other bodybuilders were doing likewise and she was starting to get turned on by the way they slathered the baby oil on themselves.

"So what do you think?" David said as he smiled and flexed for her.

"I think this is going to be one hot shoot," Annie said. The blonde male bodybuilder gave her a little wink as he oiled up his thighs.

Taking a cue from the other models, Annie grabbed some oil and began applying it to herself as well. It felt great to touch and rub her body, especially while looking at the great eye candy. She was a little surprised at herself because she was finding herself strangely drawn to the female bodybuilder. She looked at the bodybuilder's large implants and tight muscular stomach and felt herself beginning to warm up. She had never felt attracted to another woman before and was surprised at the feelings of lust she was beginning to feel towards her. The other model picked up on this and came over to her.

"Need some help with that?" she said not waiting for a reply and began applying the oil to Annie's breasts.

Annie smiled at her.

"You can help oil me, too. That is, if you want," the female bodybuilder said and smiled.

Annie hesitated for a second but then eagerly started applying oil to the bodybuilder's muscular body. She really had come a long way fast. Just a few days earlier she had been one of the most repressed people on the planet and now she was having sex with black guys and feeling lustful thoughts towards other women. What had she been thinking before? She still felt a little strange about it and was terribly afraid of getting caught, but maybe that was part of the allure? Maybe that's why it felt so good to be bad. She pushed all this out of her head because she was here to enjoy herself. She couldn't let her fears get in the way of that.

"Okay, Harold's here," David said as he walked up to them.

"Harold? You mean someone else is coming?" Annie asked, her erect nipples being oiled up under her micro-sling bikini by the strong hands of the female bodybuilder.

"Yeah, my homey, Harold Hercules. He's the one who set up the shoot. He's the one I used to play football with."

"Harold Hercules?" Annie said as her mouth automatically began to water. Wasn't that the name of the guy who Jimmy was always looking at in his muscle magazines? Wasn't that the guy she was looking at when she had broken her vow of chastity with Jimmy? It surely couldn't be.

She didn't have to wait long to find out because just a couple of seconds later, he walked in.

Annie's mouth dropped, it *was* him. He looked like a black Greek god walking up on the earth. He was like an early seventies blacksploitation movie detective with a short natural do and cowboy boots. He was also smoking a cigarillo. She got wet instantly at the sight of his rippling muscle. He was wearing a tight open-necked wide collared shirt and jeans which he promptly took off and began oiling himself up. He was completely nude and his semi-erect penis hung half-way down his muscled thigh. Annie thought that

David had been like something out of a dream, but this guy... This guy was *something else entirely*.

The female model moved in closer to her and started moving her hand down towards Annie pussy. Her breath quickened as she continued to lube Annie's body. Harold was having the same effect on her as well.

Harold noticed that she was staring at him. "This that girl you been fucking?" he said to David.

"Uh huh," David said.

"Looks good," he said and exhaled a puff of smoke.

Annie continued to stare as Harold put on his banana hammock. Her head was reeling with lust for him.

A few seconds later the photographer walked in. He was a weasely, little, older guy who looked like a pervert. Or at least Annie thought he did. She found that didn't mind this so much now. "Okay, we need to start shooting now if we're going to get this done."

They walked over to the area where he had sat up his cameras. It was near some workout mats and in front of some barbells.

"Harold, you and the new girl get together. I think that the contrast between your skin-tones would look really great against that wall."

Annie and Harold got into position and the photographer started shooting. Annie was excited to be so close to him and the photographer had been right. The contrast between her white skin and large oiled boobs and succulent hips was amazing when put next to his huge muscles and dark skin.

The photographer took a few shots and then started shaking his head. "There's something wrong."

"Am I doing something wrong?" Annie said, fully expecting her inexperience to be causing a problem.

"No, honey, it's not you. It's him," he said pointing to Harold. "He's got a hard-on that's taking over the whole shot. When people look at these pictures they won't be able to see anything else."

"I can't help it, man," Harold said sheepishly. "This girl is turning me on."

Annie quickly looked around and actually bumped into his hard-on.

"Well, until we can get it under control, we're not going to be able to do anything," the photographer said. He then looked at the other bodybuilders who were also sporting woodies. "Unless we get those dicks under control, there's no way that any reputable magazine is going to buy these shots."

"I don't know what do to then," Harold said. Then he looked at Annie. "But I think you do."

Annie didn't need another invite because she was down on her knees in a second. Harold pulled down his trunks and stepped out of them so that now he was completely nude. Annie's already hardened nipples ached to be touched and Harold obliged as she began to suck his cock. Her gorgeous body in the micro-sling bikini looked like a work of art as she got down to business. The other body builders seeing what was going on came over to them. The blonde-haired body builder and David both stepped out of their trunks and began stroking themselves around them. The female bodybuilder did likewise and began fingering her large clit. Annie was in heaven as she turned her attention to them and began to suck them each in turn. She also eagerly sucked on the female bodybuilder's clit. Everybody got a turn as she worked her way around them. Soon, however the female bodybuilder knew she was going to have to have a taste of Annie and pushed her back down onto the mat. She moved the small piece of fabric of Annie's micro sling and hungrily began eating. Annie came easily at the application of her well practiced tongue. She loved the feel of the girl's mouth on her pussy and knew that she was going to have some more of this. With her ass presented to the world, David then began fucking the female body builder. The blonde male bodybuilder and Harold stroked themselves as they watched the show.

Meanwhile, the photographer moved around them taking pictures. "Oh, yeah, oh yeah," he kept saying over and over.

Annie loved the treatment that she was getting from the female bodybuilder but she realized that she was going to have to have some cock. She then got down so that she was in prime position for doggie style. The blonde bodybuilder entered her easily, stretching her pussy with his large cock. Harold then switched out with David and began fucking the female bodybuilder who groaned with ecstasy at the feeling of his supersized member. He pounded her hard from the get-go and she fucked equally hard back. Meanwhile Annie couldn't get enough of the male blonde bodybuilder while sucking David. She couldn't believe she was doing this. It was like she was fulfilling a fantasy that she had never even known she had. She came twice with the blonde bodybuilder as he drilled her. She continued fucking them and it wasn't long before David was inside her and she was sucking the bodybuilder. She just couldn't get enough of this and she came quickly.

"I told you that you were going to have fun at the photo shoot," David said breathlessly as he rode her.

Annie couldn't answer because she was swallowing the precum of the body builder.

She continued fucking and inevitably Harold was behind her awaiting his turn. The female bodybuilder was also in front of her presenting her pussy for Annie to lick. This was just too much for Annie's body to take in and she came as Harold inserted his massive cock into her engorged vagina. He started pounding her hard and he was everything that she had imagined that he would be. He filled up every bit of her and then some. Just the thought of him inside of her was enough for her, but the fact that it was really happening was enough to make her orgasm almost immediately. He continued to fuck her hard and she was soon at the brink again. He slapped her ass occasionally as he rammed her and she couldn't believe that corporal punishment could be so wonderful. She hungrily began licking the female bodybuilder's large clit and blissfully watched as David and the male bodybuilders stood by stroking their massive erections.

"I'm going to cum again," Annie said. "I can't take it anymore!" she said as Harold continued to pound her. She had never known that sex could be so good and so dirty.

"Not yet," the female bodybuilder said and got up. Harold pulled out and allowed the female bodybuilder to get into position.

"I'm going to show you how a real bodybuilder has sex," she said and laughed. The other bodybuilders laughed too as they stroked their cocks around her.

The female bodybuilder then positioned her legs so that hers and Annie's pussies were touching. She was scissoring her and soon she began hunching Annie hard and grunting like an animal. Annie came instantly from the friction and almost bit her lip from the ecstasy of it. Her wetness and the wetness coming from the female bodybuilder's waxed vagina made for an amazing sensation. The other bodybuilders stood over them stroking their gigantic rods. Soon both she and the female bodybuilder were shaking with climax. It was then that the men blasted them with cum.

Annie felt so alive at this and of course the photographer was there capturing everything with his camera. Annie hoped that she could get copies of the prints.

But then they heard a noise. Someone had just walked into the gym.

"Annie? Annie? Are you here? I decided to surprise you." It was Jimmy and he was walking into the room carrying a bouquet of roses.

"It's my boyfriend," Annie nervously explained to the other models.

"Annie?" Jimmy said again. "What's going on?" He still hadn't gotten a good look at them.

"Jimmy?" she said, not really knowing what else to say.

Jimmy came closer and looked at her and his jaw dropped. She was coated in cum and her micro-sling bikini was moved over exposing her ripe breasts and pussy. She was wrapped around another almost nude female bodybuilder and was surrounded by David the maintenance man and the other two nude musclemen. Their semi-erect cocks were still dripping cum.

He couldn't believe his eyes and shook his head. Then he took another look. Wait a minute! he thought. Didn't that big one look familiar? It was then that he recognized him. It was the guy from his muscle magazine, Harold Hercules. It was obvious that she had just fucked all these people, the bodybuilders included. He took another look at all of them with their rippling oiled bodies. He looked at the blonde male bodybuilder and then at David and then again at Harold. Then he looked at Annie again and her large erect nipples.

"Jimmy, this isn't what it seems," she said trying to explain.

But it was too late. Jimmy's eyes rolled back in his head and he fainted flat onto the floor, dropping the bouquet.

Annie jumped up and ran over to him. The others did as well. Harold got down and felt his pulse.

"Is he dead?" Annie asked anxiously. She didn't want this to be the thing that caused her boyfriend to keel over.

"Well, he's still breathing," Harold said. "And his pulse is good."

"I think I know what's going on," the blond bodybuilder said and pointed at Jimmy's pants.

Annie looked too and breathed a sigh of relief. Jimmy had a large wet place right below his belt. Apparently the sight of all the sex and muscles had been too much for him and he had simply fainted from the overload. He had also spontaneously ejaculated all over himself. He was still noticeably aroused.

"Man, your boyfriend's got a big dick," the female bodybuilder said and began to rubbing his still erect penis. "You don't mind, do you?" she asked Annie as she unzipped his pants and fished it out and began sucking it.

"Go right ahead," Annie couldn't help but strangely feel a little bit proud of this. Her boyfriend *did* have a big cock. She really was changing. There was certainly no denying herself sexual pleasure now.

"Did you say that he was your boyfriend?" Harold said, beginning to rub his cock at the sight of the female bodybuilder sucking Jimmy's dick.

"Yeah," Annie said.

"You know, there's this party that I think the two of you would love to go to," he said.

As the female body builder worked Jimmy's cock, suddenly a loud fart erupted from Jimmy's body.

Annie groaned with embarrassment but everybody else pretended to ignore it.

The blonde bodybuilder then paused for a second and said, "Hey wait a minute, ain't that Ol' Stinky?"

14

"Harder! Harder!" Annie screamed as Jimmy breathlessly plowed into her doggie style. He was really giving it to her and was amazed that he was able to contain his jizz. He was doing so much better now since he and Annie had been doing it more often. He was very proud of himself and was so excited that each time he thrust into her, it brought him to a new level of ecstasy.

Annie on the other hand loved the feel of Jimmy's big dick deep inside of her. While he wasn't as large as David, and certainly not Harold, he did have a sizable member. Also his skinny body only enhanced the appearance of it. She was also so proud of the fact that he was really able to give it to her now without orgasming too soon. She had gotten some tips from Harold and David on how to delay his orgasm and had instructed him on what to do the next time they fucked. She was happy to see that he had listened and that the tips had worked. As for Jimmy, he was also grateful to them.

She rode his cock hard and her big breasts heaved up and down as she approached her next orgasm. She thought about her fucking at the photo shoot and it only enhanced her excitement. After Jimmy had walked in on her and had passed out from ecstasy, she knew that they had to talk. And it was one of the best talks ever.

"I'm sorry, Jimmy," she had started after he had come to.

"Oh, don't!" Jimmy had said.

"Why not? I was cheating on you," Annie said, a little confused. She had always been taught that a girl was never supposed to have sex with a man other than her husband. It only seemed right that he would be angry.

"Because this is what I've always dreamed of," he said.

"What do you mean?"

"I've always fantasized about you having sex with other guys. Especially black guys. And bodybuilders. I was always afraid to tell you about it though. I mean, before this I couldn't even think about sex without you getting angry with me."

"I know. I was so stupid," she said truthfully.

"No, you weren't stupid. You just didn't know what you were missing. You were just doing what you were taught."

"I know. But I must have been so hard on you. But it was because I didn't know any better. I promise that I'll do better in the future."

"Don't worry about that. You know better now and I have to say that it was worth the wait. I mean, when I walked in there and saw you fucking, I thought I had died and gone to heaven. I was just so happy."

"I can tell," Annie said laughing.

"Whatever you do, don't change. Don't go back. I love this. I mean, you had sex with Harold Hercules. He's my idol!"

"I'm going to fuck him again, too."

"I want to watch!"

"Sure. I would love for you to do me at the same time," she said.

"Wow!" he said and gulped. "You're finally being who you really are, Annie. Doesn't it feel good?"

"It does," Annie said.

After that discussion, their relationship had just gotten better and better. They looked at muscle magazines together and porno flicks. They had sex in public and on Jimmy's webcam. They were now truly a couple. And the sex? It was great. Jimmy was really turning into a real stud. It was like now that she was fucking all these other people, she was finally happy with him.

"Flip over," Jimmy said. "I want to see those big tits when I cum."

Dutifully, Annie obeyed. Jimmy was back inside her in a second and going full force. She rubbed her clit as he fucked her.

"Oh, Jimmy!" she said as she came.

Her writhing was too much for him and he finally had to blow. Fortunately for him, Annie was ready and stood up and hungrily took his stiff cock in her mouth to finish him off. Jimmy came a lot and after she swallowed, she looked up at him and smiled. It suddenly occurred to her that she now understood the relationship Julie had with her husband. She also felt badly over the things she had said about Julie, but regardless she was so happy.

"Do you have any sweet tea and chocolate cake?" Jimmy asked, rubbing his skinny belly. "I'm starved."

Annie winced. Jimmy may have been the perfect man for her right then, but there were still a few things they were going to have to work on.

"How about we go get some daiquiris instead?" she suggested.

Jimmy's mouth really dropped at this. She really had come a long way. Gangbanging, interracial sex, bisexuality, he could believe. But drinking alcohol? She really was beginning to let loose.

15

Alicia was just finishing up her meal at Strain's Steakhouse and Buffet while mulling over a marketing project that she was working on for class. However, she just was not able to concentrate because she couldn't get over the Annie situation. She had thought that coming here and pigging out would help to calm her mind, but it hadn't. This was surprising because eating there was something that she did sometimes to help get her mind off her problems. Strain's was the classic all-you-can-eat joint where people could pay a small price and eat all they could hold. You could also eat whatever you liked however you liked. If you liked your spaghetti and meatballs with a side order of teriyaki chicken, then you could do that. If you liked your mashed potatoes and gravy with an extra helping of french fries and hashbrowns, then Strain's was your place. Some would describe the place as a "Freeform Eaters' Paradise." Even though, oddly enough, the waitresses seemed to really dislike most of the customers because they considered anybody who ate at a restaurant "too lazy to cook," it was just a good place for people who liked to eat a lot. And also for those who weren't too picky about what they ate either.

"Hey, look, hon, it's the girl I told you about," a voice from the other side of the dining room said.

Alicia looked up. She tried hard to place the voice among the many huddled overweight people who were carrying trays and hurriedly going to their seats so they could commence with eating. Strain's was always packed and typically one had to fight just to get a place at the buffet. Especially if it was seafood night. After a couple of seconds, she was able to figure out who the voice belonged to. It was Professor Ricky and he was with a very mousy but pretty blonde haired woman with glasses. Like all the other people there, he was carrying a tray which was overloaded with extra plates and silverware. He was walking towards her table.

"Sit down," Alicia said, glad for the company.

After sitting down, Professor Ricky introduced the girl he was with as his girlfriend.

"She's a molecular biologist," he said proudly.

"I didn't know you had a girlfriend," Alicia said uneasily. She wasn't so sure about this after all. Having them sit with her could get a little uncomfortable. Especially after the fucking that Professor Ricky had given her in his office. I mean what if the girl was jealous? She might put a fork through her hand or something. Her fears were quickly put to rest, though.

"Don't you just love that dick?" she said and smiled. Her name was Professor Betty.

Alicia had to agree with her. "So you don't care that I fucked him?"

"Of course not!" Professor Betty said. "Jealousy is such a base and destructive emotion. It never accomplishes anything. I think that the pleasure you get from having sex should always override it."

"I'm certainly in agreement with that!" Professor Ricky said, chuckling goofily.

The two of them went and got their food and then sat back down. After talking for a little bit, Alicia found out that they had started dating after Julie had initially opened Professor Ricky eyes to the idea of casual sex. Because of this, he was able to gain confidence enough to ask her out. He had had a crush on her for several years but was reluctant to do anything about it because he was so inexperienced with women. After Julie had fucked him and made him aware of just what he had to offer women, he felt unstoppable and decided to ask his crush out. At first Professor Betty was a little hesitant to go out with him because she was sort of a sexual freak herself and didn't want him cramping her style.

"I thought he might be too square for me. Sexually, you know?" she said.

Alicia thought this seemed a little strange considering how dowdy and mousy she looked, but didn't say anything.

"But then I finally went out with him and took a chance. I thought I would take him back to my place and find out just how open he was. And boy was I glad I did. I figured that when I made a move on him, he would run away crying. It was a good thing I was wrong about that because, wow, when I got those pants off and saw that dick, I knew that were meant to be together."

"I can certainly understand that," Alicia said, licking her lips at the memory of the fucking she had gotten in Professor Ricky's office.

They chitchatted a little more and after dessert, Professor Betty leaned in towards Alicia.

"I hope I'm not being forward, but I was wondering if you would do something for us."

"What is it?" Alicia thought the professor might have wanted her to drop her off somewhere.

"Will you come back to my place and let me tie you up?"

"How do you mean?"

"I think you know," Professor Betty said mischievously while Professor Ricky smiled broadly.

Alicia was bit taken aback and then thought about Professor Ricky's big dick and then saw the cleavage barely visible underneath the Professor Betty's frumpy shirt and couldn't help but consent.

The two professors' cohabitated a large old Victorian house near campus which was fairly close to Strain's. They were able to get there in a matter of minutes. It wasn't long after their arrival that Alicia was completely stripped of all her clothes and Professor Betty was winding a rope around her hands, legs and ankles. They were in the bedroom and above them was a large metal hook. As Professor Betty continued to bind her, she looked up at it and wondered just what exactly was going on.

"Is this going to hurt?" she asked as Professor Betty meticulously threaded the rope around her body.

"Oh, probably a little," she said. "But you're going to love it."

"Oh," Alicia said, her breath quickening in anticipation.

After a bit more of this, Alicia was now laying face-first in the floor.

"Hoist her up, Rick," she said.

At that Alicia heard a slight whirring noise and then felt herself being raised off the ground via a pulley system. So that's what the hook had been for.

It was hard to for Alicia to see what was going on because she was facing downwards and swinging from the rope, suspended just a few feet above the floor. The ropes dug into her body just a little bit, but overall didn't feel that uncomfortable. She just felt completely helpless. As she spun slowly around the room, she could see that both Ricky and Betty were now completely nude as well. She just wondered what was going on.

She soon found out. The two professors were on her immediately. Professor Betty was on both knees and eating her out while Professor Ricky was kissing her and rubbing her boobs. She was just so helpless that she just had to let them have their way. She didn't have a choice. It was an enlightening experience to say the least. She was wet in no time as Professor Betty's skillful lips licked her pussy from to top to bottom. Professor Ricky stood up and she began sucking his erect cock. It helped stabilize her somewhat and this caused her to get even more friction with Professor Betty's mouth. They continued on for a while like this and she couldn't help but start climaxing. After this Professor Betty stopped and stood up.

"She's ready," Professor Betty said.

Professor Ricky then got behind her and entered her easily. Professor Betty held her while he began fucking her. Alicia quickly groaned with orgasm because it was such a new experience. She was just immobile and at the mercy of these two. The utter powerlessness of her situation was a complete turn-on. Soon Professor Ricky had worked up a momentum and pulled her onto him, fucking her hard. Her eyes rolled back in her head at the feeling of his big cock stretching out her wet and now slippery pussy.

After pounding her for a little bit, he stopped and Professor Betty let her go. She was just left there to swing for a couple of seconds. She was aching for more fucking.

"Aren't you going to fuck me some more?" she asked, hoping that this wasn't all they were going to do.

"Oh, yeah," Professor Betty said behind her. Professor Ricky then stepped in front of her and she eagerly took his cock in his mouth.

"Oh!" Alicia then gasped. Professor Betty had just roughly entered her with a strap-on. It was huge and Professor Betty did not bother with subtleties. She started ramming her from the get-go, slapping Alicia's ass while she nailed her pussy with the dildo.

The spanking and the fucking just drove her to the edge and she came again. Apparently it had an effect on Professor Betty as well because she came soon after from the pressure of the strap-on against her clit. Alicia could taste the precum coming up on Professor Ricky and wasn't sure if he was going to cum in her mouth or wanted to fuck her some more.

He wanted to fuck her some more.

After Professor Betty pulled out, she held Alicia steady as Professor Ricky pounded into her. He rode her hard and quick and soon came all over her restrained ass-cheeks.

They stood around for a minute afterwards, catching their breaths. Alicia was still tied up and suspended from the ceiling. They hadn't even bothered to let her go. She hoped that this was because they weren't finished with her.

"So, how did it work out with your friend? The one you were talking to me about in my office?" Professor Ricky asked.

"It didn't go too well. She's not speaking to me now. She thinks I'm just a slut," Alicia said, gently swinging.

"Ricky told me about her. You're too good for that," Professor Betty said and slapped her butt.

"OW!" Annie said.

"Yeah, you don't need her judging you. If you were around her too much, then you wouldn't ever be yourself. I know from personal experience. That's why I'm so happy I met Ricky."

"You just need to let her go," Professor Ricky said.

"I know," Alicia moaned, aching to be fucked again. It was strange that she could come to such a realization while hogtied.

16

"And then what happened?" Jimmy asked, leaning in closer to Annie.

"I pulled his cock out of his pants," Annie said matter of factly and popped a french fry into her mouth.

Annie and Jimmy were sitting in a booth at Cousin Junior's. It was lunchtime and the restaurant was crowded. She had met him on his break from the religious bookstore. They were speaking rather softly so that none of the people in the booths around them could hear them.

Annie had been on a "date" with Harold the night before and had promised to tell Jimmy all the juicy details. They had agreed that if their relationship was going to work, it was going to have to be completely open. In other words, this meant Annie could screw anybody she pleased as long as let Jimmy watch or told him the details afterwards. They hadn't really discussed what Jimmy could and couldn't do with other people sexually though. Regardless, the previous evening with Harold was her first foray into this sort of arrangement. Needless to say, it had been memorable and she was still a little horny from what had happened.

Annie had driven over to Harold's mansion which was over in the big new subdivision near the new big shopping center. Since Harold was a former pro-football player, he had plenty of money for practically whatever he wanted and he did not deny himself anything. She could definitely tell this from the size of his house and the cars in the driveway. He had a Bentley Continental and an Escalade sitting out in front. Both cars had the gold kit and were the kind of thing that only people with lots of money could afford. He also had a couple of oversized Roman style statues in his yard. It was a very classy kind of place.

Harold had invited her over to look over the pictures of the photo shoot. Of course, she knew he wanted to fuck her and she was more than happy for any excuse to see him again. He was also okay with the fact that she was only interested in sex and not a relationship.

"That's exactly what I want, baby," he had said over the phone after she had explained her situation with Jimmy to him. "I've got four ex-wives; I don't want any more of that drama."

So she had gone over to his house and had been greeted by the butler at the gigantic custom-made doors. He led her to the study and she knew that Harold had taken every effort to make the evening a special one. Harold was dressed in a leopard skin robe and silk pajama bottoms and had a magnum of Cristal on ice. "I also got some Crown Royal and other shit if you want something else," he offered.

As she looked at his chiseled chest, she was glad that she had taken the effort to dress sexily too. She wore a very short and loose black shiny dress and no panties along with a pair of high-heels. The dress was quite low-cut and since she wasn't wearing a bra, her boobs were barely contained. It had been her first time dressing like this in public and the feeling was invigorating. It was like she wasn't even wearing anything. She had just enough clothes on not to be arrested. She felt very sexy and *very* naughty.

"We'll be eating in a little bit," he said and ushered her into his vast living room to look at the pictures. As Annie walked through the house, she was amazed at the sheer beauty of it and the fine taste which Harold had exhibited in decorating. While the outside of the house had been quite grand, the inside far surpassed it in elegance and grace. The place was tiled completely in travertine with Roman inspired columns everywhere. Harold had statues of all sorts of jungle animals artfully scattered throughout the place. He had reclining jaguars and even an obsidian panther standing watch over the living room.

"These pictures turned out great," Harold said as they sat together on the sofa. His eyes and hands were all over her body as they sat down together. She didn't mind as he gently massaged her thigh as they looked at the pictures. She had to admit that the pictures did look good. While the pictures of the actual fitness modeling were there, what she and Harold were most interested in were the shots the photographer had taken of the sex.

"When you did that," Harold said pointing to a picture of her thrusting against him, "I thought I was going to lose my damn mind." She thought the same thing about herself, remembering how it had felt fucking someone as big and muscled as he was.

Of course, it didn't take much longer for Harold's hand to move from Annie's thigh to her pussy and of course she was already wet. She had thought that they would eat dinner first before fucking, but this would be a great way to work up an appetite. Besides, they would probably fuck again before she left.

They talked for a while as he rubbed between her legs and she reached over and started stroking his big cock through his pajamas. She could feel every contour of his penis through the silky fabric.

It wasn't long before Annie was so turned on that she was leaving a wet patch on the sofa and Harold's massive member ached to be free.

"Baby, let's cut the shit and fuck."

Annie was happy that he was so forward with what he wanted. Especially when it was what she wanted too.

She got down on her knees in front of him and pulled his pajama bottoms down and began sucking the head of his cock. It was so big and so hard that she had a hard time getting more than the head in her mouth, but as she worked the tip, she could feel Harold's body tensing. When he did this, she knew that she was definitely doing something right. She was getting better and better at this. He reached under her dress and rubbed her boobs as she sucked. She rubbed her clit with one hand as she worked his cock with her lips and mouth. She was aching to be fucked and when she began to taste precum, she knew that it was time.

"Not yet, baby," he said and picked her up like a ragdoll and sat her down on the sofa and raised her dress and began licking her pussy. His tongue felt so good and he licked her up and down, sucking her clit, quickly bringing her to orgasm.

She stepped out of her dress and climbed up on top of him so she was straddling him. She grabbed his cock and guided it into her engorged vagina.

"Oh, yeah," he said as his cock slid into her easily.

Harold sucked her tits as she ground against him and rode him. Her hands held his muscled chest as she went up and down on him harder and harder. She marveled at the contrast of his darkness against her whiteness and couldn't get enough of looking at his rockhard abs. Even though she had gigantic boobs she looked tiny against him. She climaxed quickly and then started working on another as he picked up momentum. She has such a full feeling in her pussy that she came again quickly. It was such a good feeling fucking him. She had to work a little bit for the orgasm with Jimmy, but with Harold it was like she had subscribed to orgasm on demand.

"Do me doggie," she said and got up off him. She sucked his cock a little before she got on all fours, becoming even more aroused at the taste of herself on him.

She got into position on the sofa and Harold got behind her, one knee on the sofa and the other on the floor and he began fucking her hard. He was not holding back and Annie felt another orgasm come quickly. She moaned loudly because she knew that Harold was not messing around.

"Go ahead and cum," she said hungering for the taste of his jizz.

He just kept pounding her. He was like a machine. A fucking machine.

"You better get ready, gal," he said breathlessly as he brought himself to orgasm. "Because I'm going to shoot all over this motherfucker."

"Oh, I'm ready," she said.

He slowed and she felt him tensing again. She quickly got down on her knees and took his cock in her mouth. He stroked himself as she licked the head.

"Yeah, baby. Lick that damn dick," he said and began to cum, coating her lips and mouth.

She moved her tongue around her mouth, licking up as much as she could.

After they caught their breath, the butler came in and announced that dinner was ready.

As Annie told her story, Jimmy was so horny by this point that he could have started jerking off right there in Cousin Junior's. "And what did you have?" he asked eagerly.

"Oh, we had roast goose, a ham, a turkey and all sorts of green beans and stuffing and a pineapple upside down cake and a baked Alaska.

"Wow!" Jimmy said.

"He said that he hadn't gone to that much effort with the food because he knew we were going to have sex most of the night anyway," she added. "He also invited me to a party at somebody named Cornbread's place. He had invited me at the photo shoot, but was just reminding me. I think Cornbread lives in the same neighborhood as him or something."

"Are we going?"

"Sure. He said that we would have fun. He said that Cornbread was hung."

"Sounds like a good time. And what did you do after dinner?" Jimmy asked excitedly.

"Well, we had sex for the rest of the night."

Jimmy was almost salivating by this point. "So are you going to tell your mom?" he asked, his hard-on was now so large his pants could barely contain it. The head was just beginning to peep up over his waistband.

"I'm not telling her anything. All she would do is just make me feel bad about myself."

"Well, good then let's go back to your apartment and fuck," Jimmy said.

"I knew there was a reason why I made two gallons of sweet tea this morning," Annie said grinning.

"Well, let's go!" Jimmy jumped up ecstatically. "I'm awfully thirsty."

17

"Oh, yes, fuck me harder, you sight-reading bastard!"

Annie's mother was leaning over the arm of her floral sofa and getting it hard from her church's Music Director.

"You're really making my choir sing!" she said as he plowed into her. She was a little bit stoned because she was smoking a joint while he fucked her. That only enhanced her enjoyment because if there's one thing she enjoyed, it was fucking while buzzed. Even when Annie's father had been alive she had enjoyed an extra fuck on the side, but the pot? Well, the pot just capped it off.

The Music Director who was about ten years younger than Annie's mother had a surprisingly large penis. This is why Annie's mother had put her hooks into him. If she was going to go cougaring, it was going to be after a cub who was packing. He looked like your typical music director with his hair-sprayed pompadour, moustache and ever present smile. Also like most music directors he hadn't thought twice when Annie's mother had asked him over. He knew what her game was and only wondered what had taken her so long.

He pounded her good and he knew he was hitting her g-spot when she dug in and started grunting like an animal.

"Ugh! Ugh!" she said, ramming against him as he fucked her hard.

Of course, after two hours of hard fucking the Music Director was almost finished. He just couldn't keep up with Annie's mother's raw sexuality. Besides, he had to go to choir practice.

"I'm going to cum!" he yelled, completely pitch perfect.

"Well, give me the full load!" she said and started bumping up against him so hard that he almost lost his balance.

Annie's mother started grinning as she felt his hot gism squirting deeply into her pussy. They were just getting dressed when the door opened.

"Mom?"

It was Annie and she had caught them in the act. Or immediately after, rather. She couldn't believe it. Her mother and the Music Director? She was shocked and just stood there, not knowing what to do. This was like finding out that there was no Santa Claus or Easter Bunny for her. Here she had gone through her life thinking that her mother was one way and then she had found out that she was another way completely. She just didn't know what to say.

"Is that the Music Director from church?" she finally managed to say. The Music Director was standing there, still parially nude, his erection slowly deflating. He continued to smile sheepishly while slowly backing out of the room.

Annie's mother just rolled her eyes and finished putting on her housecoat. "Of course it is." Then she shrugged. "Oh, come on! Don't act like a baby. We're just fucking."

"But Mom! After all you've said about people who do this kind of thing. And you're smoking a marijuana cigarette, too! You even smell like you've been drinking!"

"Well, I'll be going now," the Music Director said grabbing his clothes and starting out the door. "It was nice seeing you again, Annie." He left quickly.

"You too," Annie replied without thinking. After all, she had been raised to be polite.

"I'll see you in church on Sunday," Annie's mother yelled lustily after him. "And after church as well," she cackled.

"I just can't believe you." Annie was truly disappointed. Here she had been hiding her newfound sexuality from everyone she knew because she was afraid of her mother and now she was finding out that her mother was probably an even bigger slut than she was. She had made her life so much harder than it had to be. She felt very foolish and very misled.

At this point, her mother beckoned her over to sit on the couch. "Let me tell you a few things, Annie."

The two of them sat down.

"I know I owe you an explanation, but I always thought you knew about me. I always thought that you knew all this goody two-shoes stuff was just an act."

"But what about Cheerfully Chaste? You were a sponsor for crying out loud!"

Annie's mother started chuckling. "I thought everybody looked at it as a joke. Nobody can really stick with a program like that. I mean, who would want to? I thought you knew that no one could possibly be this good and pure."

"No, Mom, I didn't. I thought it was for real. I lived my life by the pledge and it's caused me to be really weird and to be mean and judge people. I don't really appreciate it. Why did you do it? Why did you act like this if you really weren't like this?"

Annie's mother sighed. "It's like this. I grew up in a very small town. In that town, everybody knew everybody's business and every single person there acted like they were so pure that they had never heard of sex or alcohol or anything that could be construed as making them an immoral person. Sure, they had some wild spells when they were in their teens but when they grew up a little bit, they would once again start acting like they were back in middle school. You had to be pure or you were looked at some sort of dirty bird. The purer you acted and the more you judged other people, the better you would look. Also people wouldn't judge you nearly as much if you were the one who was pointing the finger."

"But everybody wasn't really like that, were they?"

"Oh, hell no!" Her mother laughed. "Everybody just acted like that. People fucked everybody else's wives and husbands. The preacher even got drunk and screwed the deacon's wives. It was a lot of fun. You just couldn't talk about it. If you did, they would turn on you and then make your life hell. Why the biggest whore in town would get up in church and call you a slut if you didn't keep it hidden. It was all sort of like a game or something."

"It sounds more like a mental illness."

"Yeah, I can see that. But that's the way a lot of people are."

"But Mom, you don't live in that town anymore."

"I know. Old habits die hard."

Annie thought for a minute. "But you don't think you would be happier just being open about who you really are? A woman who loves sex?"

"Probably. I never thought about it," she said truthfully. "I always figured that people would think badly of you if they knew what you were really like."

"Did Dad know about you?"

She started laughing. "Heck yeah," he did. "He was like this too. He couldn't keep it in his pants."

Annie was silent for a minute. She was mulling over doing something she had never dreamed of doing before she had had this talk with her mother.

"Mom, I think we should start being honest with each other."

"Sure," she said.

"I think you should start being open and stop acting like you're something you're not."

"But what will people think?"

"It doesn't matter. People should like you for what you are rather than what you're not."

"Really?" Annie's mother said.

"Really." And then Annie took the first step by telling her mother just what she had been up to lately.

"I told you that's what would happen at your little photo shoot," her mother said in her old judgmental way and then laughed. Annie couldn't help but laugh too.

18

Alicia was sitting on a bench in front of the library at college thinking about what Professor Ricky and Professor Betty had said to her about her situation and realized that she was going to have to let Annie go. As hard as it was to think about, she knew it was true. Since she really didn't have anyone else to talk to that would understand, she called up Julie. She was still out in California and volunteering at the Cardboard Cathedral with Brother Red Hair.

"It's just impossible," she said tearfully as she spoke to Julie on the phone. "She's never going to change! She's just too much of a prude!"

"Well, at least you tried," Julie said consolingly. "Some people are just harder to turn out that others. I was pretty easy, but then again the guy who did it to me really knew what he was doing."

"It's too bad he's not around now," Alicia said wistfully.

"It probably still wouldn't work. I mean Annie is just *too* uptight. She's just not willing to accept that other people think differently than her. I wasn't really like that. I was naïve, but I wasn't close-minded."

"It just hurts that we can't be friends anymore," Alicia said. "I really miss her and I miss telling her things. I just wish we could still hang out together, but she's just so judgmental."

"You don't need that in your life. You don't need her making you feel bad about yourself. Just be polite to her when you see her and move on. It happens in life. Not everybody stays friends forever. "

"I know that's what I need to do."

"And you need to get fucked. As often and by as many people as possible," Julie said, trying to cheer her up.

"Well, I've been working on that," Alicia said and went on to tell her all about what she had been up to as did Julie.

They talked for a little while longer and then hung up. Alicia felt much better after talking to Julie. She wished that she could be here with her during this time, but understood that she had important work to do on the West Coast.

She agreed that if she was going to get over this thing with Annie she was going to have to be true to herself and get fucked as much as possible. Cock and a lot of it would cure her of her blues. She was definitely feeling better but then her thoughts were suddenly interrupted by the sound of a motorcycle roaring up and popping a wheelie on the sidewalk behind her. Then the rider started doing donuts around her park bench and creating a real ruckus. She was a little frightened by what was going on, but then noticed that Campus Security was just sitting across from her in a squad car. She tried to wave at them to get their attention, but they didn't act like they saw her. They just sat and watched the motorcyclist and didn't even attempt to do anything about his obviously illegal behavior.

The motorcyclist then stopped and pulled behind her and stopped and took off his helmet. It was Cornbread. Of course. She breathed a sigh of relief.

"You still bringing your hot ass to my party tomorrow?"

Annie smiled. "Definitely."

"Well, get ready to get fucked. Everybody has a good time at Cornbread's!" he whooped, referring to himself in the third person and revving up his motorcycle and then roared off.

"So I've heard," Alicia said to herself. Her outlook was improving already.

19

"Come on in, you motherfuckers!" Cornbread yelled over the music. He was dressed as a quasi-race car driver. He was carrying a trophy and was accompanied by two stacked blondes; however he was only wearing a baseball cap and a black and white checkered banana hammock. "And grab something to drink! If you ain't drinking, you ain't welcome at my damn party! Yee haw!"

As expected, Cornbread's party was in full swing much to the annoyance of all his neighbors except Harold, who was also in attendance at the party. It was a summer costume soiree and everyone, except for Cornbread that is, was required to wear masks. He reasoned that people needed to know who he was so they would know that they were at the right party. Which sort of made sense and was very considerate of him, but who else in the neighborhood would have such an over-the-top costume party? However, no one had said that Cornbread was the brightest guy in the world. Still, everybody loved ol' Cornbread.

Since all Cornbread's parties, regardless of the theme, ended up as orgies, people were fairly scantily dressed. Harold walked around completely nude with a Lone Ranger style mask and cape. He called himself, "The Black Cock Hero" and really hammed it up.

"I'm here to rescue all the women from the world of tiny dicks," he jokingly said many times to everybody he ran into and smoked his cigarillo and drank from a Waterford crystal champagne flute. He had brought his own because he didn't really like drinking from the plastic cups that Cornbread had provided. He didn't think it looked dignified.

As Annie walked around in her skimpy Cinderella outfit and mask, she realized that there had been so much in life that she had been sheltered from. Her skirt was high and she wore no panties. Even though she was hanging out of her costume because her boobs were barely contained by the dress, she still felt a little overdressed. Most of the other girls there were in micro-sling bikinis or pasties. While she had never been to a sex party before, she knew that how this night was going to end up. She could just feel it. In a way, it was very similar to the cakewalks and ice cream socials she had attended all her life, except at this party, people were drinking alcohol and were barely clothed. She also enjoyed the anonymity that her mask provided. It allowed her to really cut loose without everybody judging her and calling her a hypocrite. She could also tell that all eyes were on her and that they were trying to figure out who she was.

"I got you a daiquiri," Jimmy said coming up beside her and handing her a plastic cup. He was dressed as a leprechaun with a matching green bowler hat, banana hammock and suspenders.

"Thanks," she said, still surveying the room.

"I almost couldn't find you," Jimmy said to her. "There are just too many people here."

"I know. It's great isn't it?"

"Hey, look there's David!" Jimmy said excitedly and pointed across the room.

"No, that's Harold," Annie said.

"No, over there's Harold," Jimmy said pointing over to the other side of the room.

Apparently David was dressed, or rather undressed exactly the same as Harold except with a red cape instead of a black one.

David came over to them. Annie's eye instantly went to his semi-hard dick. She couldn't help but reach out and stroke it a little.

"Harold stole my damn idea!" David said hotly. "I was supposed to be The Black Cock Hero! Now there are two of us! Shit!"

"Maybe you could team up?" Annie said still stroking his cock, loving the way it was getting hard in her hand.

"I guess so," David said sullenly. "He's just pissing me off. He's always doing that shit. Stealing my ideas."

"Well, it doesn't matter, you both look great," Jimmy said enthusiastically.

David gave Jimmy a sideways glance and then turned to Annie. "Well, I've got to go mingle. I'll be catching you later." he said and winked.

Annie winked back. "I hope so."

As time went by and people drank more and more, everyone began to start loosening up and start having sex. It started out in a small way as it usually does. Someone started sucking someone's dick or maybe a couple started having sex out by the pool or in the hot tub, but pretty soon everybody finally got the idea that it was time for the party to really start.

Outside the house Alicia was no exception. She had arrived late to the party due to a project she was working on for school and was just getting there after the sex had started. She had come as the Queen of Hearts and for a costume she had just worn a red mask and a heart-themed microkini that she had found at Elizabeth's Misadventure. It was so tiny that it barely covered her nipples. She might as well not even been wearing any bottoms because most of her ass was showing and her pussy was just slightly concealed by a tiny red heart. Her red high-heels only served to set the outfit off. She found herself getting horny as she walked around the pool area, seeing people involved in all sorts of sexual situations. It was like an orgy but on a bigger scale as it was spread out all over the house. She walked into the house and immediately saw the tree trimmers tag-teaming a hot redhead. They waved at her and then high-fived each other. She smiled and waved back and then continued on. She was trying to find Cornbread because wanted to try that big dick of his. She didn't have to look far because she could hear him hooting and hollering over the loud music that was blasting. She walked into that room and saw him getting his dick sucked by a sexy black girl. She also saw the two lesbians, April and Sunny, involved in a daisy chain with the two girls that had been part of Cornbread's racecar themed costume. She waved at them and they smiled in acknowledgement.

"Shit! You came!" Cornbread said recognizing Alicia. "That's a great costume too. You need to get out of it as soon as possible!"

Alicia undid her bikini and walked over to him and bent down and joined the black girl in sucking his dick. It was a huge thing and there was more than enough for her and the black girl to share. He definitely lived up to the hype. He really was hung. She was on her knees in the middle of the living room sucking his cock in the midst of loads of other people having sex. She just couldn't believe it. It was crazy. But she felt like she belonged. She also felt like she was home here and this feeling only made her want to get fucked even more so.

After a little more sucking, she turned and presented her pussy so Cornbread could have easier access to her pussy. He began licking it and the black girl moved on over to another cock.

"Mmmm...that pussy tastes like it needs to be fucked," he said.

"It does," she said.

With that, Cornbread rose up and slowly inserted his massive dong into her slippery vagina doggie style. It was tough fitting him all the way in, but he finally got there. Alicia's eyes rolled back in her head as he hit every single square millimeter of the interior of her pussy. It had never been stretched like this before, not even with the ten-inch jelly dong or with Buzz at the adult book store. She just writhed on him and had an orgasm immediately. He was so big that he couldn't help but hit her g-spot with every thrust.

As she fucked him, she noticed another pussy directly in front of her. It belonged to a girl who was bent over and sucking the massive dick of a black guy wearing a red cape while a skinny white guy licked her tit and jerked off. Her pussy was so close that she couldn't help but reach out and start stroking it. The girl responded and moved closer to her and soon Alicia was licking it. It tasted good too and it just made Alicia want to grind against Cornbread's massive cock even more.

"Keep eating my pussy," the girl in front of her said. "Just lick it."

Alicia stopped fucking for a second. She recognized that voice.

"Don't stop. Just keep licking it," the voice said again.

"Annie?" Alicia said and then groaned as Cornbread rammed her.

Surprised, the girl in front of her turned around suddenly. She still held onto the fully erect black cock though. She didn't want it to get away, apparently. "Alicia?"

"But....?!" Alicia was speechless. She was just so flabbergasted that she couldn't believe it. She didn't know whether she wanted to be angry at Annie's hypocrisy or happy at the idea that her friend had loosened up. Around them, people stopped fucking and watched the exchange.

"This is awkward," Annie said, taking her mask off and continuing to stroke David's dick.

"I'll say it is! Who would have thunk it?" Jimmy said, grinning and leering at Alicia's nude body.

"Jimmy? You too?" Alicia said. Then she looked at his large penis. "You're that hung?" she said and bit her lip as Cornbread pounded her again.

"Hey, you're that stuck up little piece of ass from the mall, ain't you?" Cornbread said, grinning and slapping Alicia on the ass. He was on cruise control as he continued to fuck Alicia while observing the situation.

"And you're that big dicked redneck, aren't you?" Annie said stuck out her tongue at him.

"Shit yeah!" Cornbread said and pumped into Alicia.

"You mean your friends didn't know?" David said in amazement, rubbing the end of his dick. "About you getting all wild and shit? They still thought you was still a goody-two-shoes?"

"You mean *this* girl's a goody-two-shoes?" Harold said. He had just walked up. He semi-erect cock dangled in front of Alicia. "Man, this girl is an absolute freak!"

"Really?" Alicia said eyeing Harold's large crank while being gently fucked by Cornbread.

Harold gave her a look that suggested that he was indeed telling the truth.

"I guess goody's gone bad then," April said joining in on the conversation.

"Wow!" Alicia said. She just didn't know what to think.

Annie reached out patted on the arm. "Let's talk about this later. Everything is okay. Let's just say that you were right. I was wrong. Let's start fucking."

And that's all it took.

Annie backed up beside Alicia and Cornbread started rubbing her pussy. All the guys stood around them stroking their hard-ons as Cornbread side-by-sided them, fucking Alicia and then switching over to Annie. Both the girls started taking turns sucking the cocks in front of them. Alicia was amazed at how big Jimmy's cock was and was still very shocked that she was sucking on it. Annie was in turn amazed at how big Cornbread's dick was. It was like a different experience from what she had felt before. She still preferred Harold's big black one, but this one was nothing to sneeze at. April and Sunny went back to their puppy pile but still kept an eye on the festivities going on with Alicia and Annie.

After a while of fucking and after both girls had orgasmed several times, Cornbread pulled out.

"I got an idea about goody-goody here, boys. I think we need to make her air-tight!"

Annie looked up puzzledly. "What's that?"

"Just sit back and relax and let us show you," Harold said, smiling.

"Well, okay, then," Anne said.

Cornbread then lay back on the floor. "Just crawl up on top of my dick."

Alicia watched the spectacle and was beginning to get even more aroused. Just seeing her friend in this situation had her almost on overload. She pulled David in next to her. Since he was always in search of new pussy, he began rubbing her tits while they watched.

Annie crawled on top of Cornbread and inserted his massive dong into her pussy. Then before she knew it,

Harold was behind her pressing his big black dick into her ass. She was so slippery from fucking that he was able to get in fairly easily.

Annie gasped at the feeling and became even more turned on. This was her first anal experience and she was surprised at how easily Harold had been able to get into her. She was born for this, she realized. She was so full that she couldn't believe it. She climaxed immediately and began thrusting, her big tits rising up and down as she moved. She was astonished to feel that however she moved she was getting dick pushed into her. Double penetration was truly moving experience for her.

"Boyfriend, now you get in front of her so she can suck you," Cornbread said.

Jimmy dutifully obeyed and when Annie began hungrily sucking his penis, Harold couldn't help but yell, "Airtight!"

Annie had found out what airtight meant all right. Three big cocks plugging every hole. Any way she moved she had cock in her. In her mouth, in her ass and in her pussy. She was a happy girl and just started writhing as the men began to fuck her. She was completely at their disposal.

"Oh, yeah!" Jimmy said as Annie sucked him and watched Cornbread and Harold fuck her. Annie ground against Cornbread and backed into Harold, meanwhile deepthroating Jimmy. He had never dreamed something like this existed. If she had been able to speak, Annie would have yelled to the world, "I couldn't feel dirtier! And I love it!" However, her mouth was full so all she could do was slurp on Jimmy's big dick.

As Alicia watched, she realized that couldn't take any more.

"Put that big black cock in me," she said to David. She stood up and he backed her against a bookcase and immediately got her into the stork position, licking her erect nipples as they fucked.

It wasn't long before everybody had had all the pleasure they could handle and pulled out of Annie. They gathered around her and started ejaculating on her, coating her with cum. She laughed as she rubbed her fingers in it and licked them clean. She watched as Alicia continued to get pounded by David. She smiled when she saw David start pumping really hard and then thrust deep into her, filling her pussy with cum.

After was over and Cornbread and Harold had high-fived each other, Alicia went over to Annie.

"We've got to call Julie," Alicia said.

"That would be great," Annie said. "Especially now that we've got so much in common."

20

"Wasn't I right?" Annie said as she snapped a picture of Alicia fucking Harold. She was taking the pictures at Cornbread's place in the formal dining room. The room was filled with the sounds and smells of sex and it was difficult for her to be heard over the moaning. She repeated herself so that she could be heard.

"I'll say," Alicia said, biting her lip, in between thrusts. "He is good." She was leaned over the dining table while Harold stood behind her. Jimmy was still at work selling religious tracts but promised to drop by later.

"Ain't as good as me!" Cornbread piped in, walking into the room, hard-on raging and drinking a beer.

"Now don't talk about me like I ain't here," Harold said and laughed, pumping into Alicia. "Just make sure you get my good side."

And so it turned out that the two friends had become even better friends than they were before. After Cornbread's party they had a long talk about the situation. Both girls had apologized for their behavior and intolerance. Alicia hadn't really done anything but she did feel awful for writing Annie off as a friend. Annie felt badly about everything and pledged that she would never judge anybody again. She also said that she would always be true to herself and not care what anybody thought. Alicia understood completely the pressure that joining Cheerfully Chaste had placed on them and how as a result, Annie had felt that she had to live a lie in order to be accepted.

Alicia had been amazed to find out about Annie's mother, but somehow in the back of her mind she was not surprised. There had always been something about her that hadn't rung true and Alicia just realized that this was just a case of her instincts being right, even though at the time, she hadn't understood what her instincts were telling her. She was just happy to see that Annie's mother was now going to swing parties and had even vacationed at a nudist resort. She still wasn't openly being a slut like she and Annie were doing, but she knew that she would in time. She was still a rather old-fashioned woman and would have to start out gradually.

The two girls were even closer now that they could literally do anything they pleased without being judged by each other. They didn't really care what anybody else thought because they had nothing to gain if people they didn't know or care about thought badly of them. All they were concerned about was what made them feel good and if people really loved and cared about them they would want them to be happy. Regardless of what they did sexually. It was a way of finding out who their real friends were, so to speak.

Of course, Julie had been ecstatic at the news. "See I told you," she said to Alicia. "Everybody wants to do this stuff. They're just too afraid to try. But once they do, watch out!" She called Annie and said that she didn't have any hard feelings and that she was really proud of her. This made Annie very happy.

"Hold that pose," Annie said as Harold went balls deep into Alicia's pussy. She tried as hard as she could, but the sheer size of him that deep in her made her start trembling with climax.

"That's good," Annie said, but then turned around fast. Cornbread had slapped her on the ass hard. She had stopped wearing panties so there was nothing to cushion the blow. She knew that she was going to have a handprint on her ass from it.

"I'm ready to fuck," Cornbread said proudly. He was now completely nude and Annie instantly was turned on by his rock-hard tattooed body and fully erect skyscraper-like penis.

She put the camera down on the table and got down on both knees and started sucking him, filling her mouth with his cock. She sucked him for a little and then realized that she wanted to be fucked, too. She leaned over the dining room table and raised her skirt so that there would be no impediment to Cornbread getting inside her.

Now she was side by side with her friend and they were both getting fucked by two good-looking big dicked guys. This was the kind of things that friends should do. They smiled at each other as they got fucked. Annie thrust against Cornbread, trying to get every inch of him into her. She came fast but he still kept fucking her hard.

"Let's switch," Annie said.

"Sure," Alicia said.

Harold and Cornbread switched places and it wasn't long before both girls were cumming again.

"Come on and cum," Alicia said to the guys.

"Sure thing!" Cornbread said.

Both girls got down on their knees while Harold squirted his big black dick and Cornbread his huge white one all over them. Their faces were coated with cum and they couldn't help but start laughing. Harold and Cornbread went to get drinks while the two girls went into the bathroom to clean up.

"This is a long way from Cheerfully Chaste," Annie said, wiping the cum off her breasts and tasting it.

"And that darn pledge, Alicia added, washing her face.

"I think we need a new one," Annie said.

"I do too."

"Let me think," Annie said, looking up at the ceiling, trying to come up with something.

"Oh I know, Alicia said.

"I think I know where you're going," Annie said.

"We must cheerfully *never* deny ourselves pleasure," they said together and cracked up.

This was one pledge that both girls vowed never to break.